HER KIND-HEARTED BILLIONAIRE

JULIETTE DUNCAN

BILLIONAIRES WITH HEART CHRISTIAN ROMANCE

"I enjoyed this warmly written clean romance between a billionaire and school teacher who met on a missions trip to Thailand. The romance slowly blossomed, grew, and the characters matured and overcame their fears and life's circumstances. " ~ *Gail*

"I just finished this book and it is wonderful. Juliette has a way of making her characters really lifelike. And, in this book, she also captures the awfulness of human trafficking. I felt like I was right there. It's a beautifully written book of how Good can work in even the most unexpected people."~*Mary*

"I love Juliette Duncan books. They are down to earth, dealing with real life situations. Not to forget to mention, a Christian perspective. Clean and well written. This book is absolutely no exception. I loved the premise of a billionaire searching for more for his life. " ~ *Robin*

"Juliette Duncan has written a sweet, tender romance while dealing with the horrible situation of child sex trafficking, without any graphic details. I adored both of the well-developed main characters, Nick and Phoebe." ~*Lisa*

FOREWORD

HELLO! Thank you for choosing to read this book - I hope you enjoy it! Please note that this story is about a billionaire, Nicholas Barrington, and a grieving young woman, Phoebe Halliday, both from Australia. Australian spelling and terminology have been used and are not typos!

As a thank you for reading this book, I'd like to offer you a FREE GIFT. That's right - my FREE novella, "Hank and Sarah - A Love Story" is available exclusively to my newsletter subscribers. Go to http://www.julietteduncan.com/subscribe to get the ebook for FREE, and to be notified of future releases.

I hope you enjoy both books! Have a wonderful day!

Juliette

CHAPTER 1

*S*ydney, Australia

Nicholas Barrington sat behind his desk on the forty-fifth floor of the tower bearing his family's name and removed his pre-prepared meal from his lunch bag. Below, Sydney Harbour shimmered in the midday sun and looked spectacular. A small tugboat, looking much like a toy from this height, guided a large cruise ship through the harbour towards the heads, while a number of yachts sliced through the water easily in what Nick assumed was a strong breeze, given the trim of their sails. The problem was, being on the forty-fifth floor, he was removed from reality. The view was sensational, but he felt like a spectator. He'd much rather be a participant.

A firm knock sounded on his office door, pulling his gaze from the vista. Nicholas swivelled around. Alden, his brother and fellow director, sauntered in and sank into the chair on the opposite side of the desk. "Taking time for lunch today, bro?"

At thirty-one, Alden was two years younger than Nicholas and had the same sea-blue eyes, although his hair was lighter.

"Yes. I was just about to eat. Did you bring yours?" For a moment, Nicholas forgot he was talking with his brother. Of course Alden hadn't brought his lunch.

Alden scoffed, eyeing Nicholas's bag with amusement. "It'll be here in five minutes."

Nicholas pulled out his sandwich and salad, glad he didn't have to wait for his meal to be delivered.

"Eating in here today?" Charity, their younger sister, appeared in the doorway. The sharp bob framing her pixie-like face was the same dark colour as his, but she had their late mother's emerald green eyes. She plopped onto the chair next to Alden and pulled a portable blender filled with green powder from her carry bag. Opening a bottle of water, she poured half of it in and hit the button.

"That looks disgusting," Nicholas shouted over the whir of the machine.

"Try some if you like."

Grimacing, he quickly shook his head. "No thanks. I'll stick to my sandwich."

Moments later, a young man knocked tentatively on the door holding a rectangular food box. Alden waved him in and took the box.

Setting it on the desk, he peeled back the cardboard lid, revealing a large steak with new potatoes and green beans. Although it smelled appetising, as Nicholas took the last bite of his sandwich and moved onto the salad, he was thankful his tastes weren't the same as his siblings. He was a simple man with simple needs.

"It's all right, but it could be better," Alden commented after swallowing his first mouthful.

Nicholas ignored his brother's comment and instead focused on Charity who'd just turned the blender off. The silence was very welcome.

"So, you know I was meant to be flying to Bali tomorrow for that meditation retreat?" Angling her head, she glanced at him as she poured some of the green concoction into a glass.

He nodded. Of late, Charity had been delving into meditation and something about self-praise and how to be her own deity. Not what Nicholas would have considered a worthwhile venture, but, each to his own. He'd started exploring things of a spiritual nature as well, but his initial explorations had led him to a traditional church, although he hadn't yet made up his mind whether that was what he wanted.

"Looks like I'll have to postpone the flight to another day." Charity released a frustrated sigh before taking a mouthful of what Nicholas considered a disgusting looking green concoction.

"Why's that?"

"Why?" Charity's green eyes bulged. "Because of that lazy pilot." Her voice rose to a crescendo and Nicholas wouldn't have been surprised if the whole floor had heard.

"Ugh, don't even get me started." Alden shook his head, waving a fork in the air.

Charity leaned forward. "Can you believe he told me he can't work tomorrow? I mean, I'm his boss. It's not like we're ordering him to fly every day. He gets plenty of time off. I just needed him for one day."

"Why can't he take you?" Nicholas asked in a calm voice.

"His daughter's having surgery. I get that family is important and all that, but honestly, it's only a few hours each way. He'd be back before she even woke up."

Nicholas studied his sister with sadness. He doubted she knew that Roger's small daughter had been born with special needs and her surgeries required extensive preparation. Even the anesthesia was a risk. But it was no use saying anything. She wouldn't understand or care. "Did he suggest anyone else who could step in?"

"I don't want anyone else. They wouldn't know our plane like he does." Charity blew out another breath and sipped her concoction. "Anyway, I think we should fire him." Shifting in her chair, she crossed her long, slim legs and adjusted her skirt.

"I agree," Alden said. "Last time he took me to Dubai, we were an hour late. He said it was because they didn't have a place for us to land, but isn't it his job to make sure all of that's figured out ahead of time?"

Nicholas sighed. "That's hardly his fault. Sometimes unexpected things happen that are out of anyone's control. You know Roger's competent and he always does his best."

"You're so naive, big brother. You always want to see the good in everybody. No wonder they take advantage of you." Alden gave him a withering look.

Nicholas pursed his lips. He wished his siblings could show a little more humility and understanding, especially since they'd been given so much. How could they be so cruel and selfish when it came to others?

Taking a sip from his water bottle, Nicholas shut out his siblings as they continued talking about things he couldn't relate to. Although the three were very different, it saddened

4

him they weren't closer. Without any other family, they only had each other. But all they ever talked about was the business and what gave them pleasure, like Charity's Bali trip. Beyond that, very little of depth ever entered their conversations. While the two continued to talk about things of no interest to him, Nicholas returned to his work, but his ears pricked when Alden mentioned their late grandfather, James Barrington.

"You know, old James wouldn't have liked us wasting the money on a lousy staffer. Just because a man's nice enough doesn't make him worth the money." It seemed they'd returned to the issue of whether to fire Roger or not. Nicholas groaned. From what he remembered of James Barrington, firing a man because of an important family issue would have been the last thing he would have done.

When he died, the three siblings had inherited their grandfather's fortune, amassed during the mining boom of the eighties. A billion for each, plus the company divided between them. Now the trio lacked for nothing, but as much as Nicholas appreciated the life he now had, he would much have preferred his grandfather, and his parents, to still be alive. How different things would have been if his parents had inherited instead of the three grandchildren.

He sighed sadly. Yes, he'd give just about anything to have his parents back. It didn't seem fair that their lives had been snuffed out while they were still in their prime.

"So, do you think we should fire him? After he takes me to Bali, of course?" Charity asked nonchalantly, inspecting her perfectly manicured nails.

"Don't be a fool," Alden said harshly.

For a moment, Nicholas held hopes that his brother might

stick up for the man, but they were soon dashed when Alden continued. "You should probably wait until he brings you back from Bali. You don't want to be stuck there!" He laughed, and Charity joined in.

Nicholas seethed. He had to say something, but he needed to remain calm and rational. An emotional defense of the pilot wouldn't go over well with his siblings. "Why don't we give him another chance? His daughter is having surgery, it's hardly a time to be selfish."

Charity huffed with exasperation. "Whatever you say, big brother. Although I don't see how it affects you, since you never use the private jet, anyway." Her voice dripped with sarcasm.

Biting his lip, Nicholas brushed her comments and attitude off. They'd soon forget about the pilot and move on to a discussion about shoes or something as equally trivial.

"Well, I'm headed out. I've got a hot yoga class this afternoon." Charity stood, tossed her rubbish in the bin, and then picked up her blender.

"Don't you need more than that shake before working out?" Alden waved the last piece of steak on his fork as if he were teasing her with it.

She rolled her eyes. "Keep your cow, thanks." With that, she turned and left the room, teetering on her stilettos.

Alden mopped up the last of his gravy, said a brief goodbye to Nicholas, and then also left the office.

Leaning back in his chair, Nicholas released a slow breath and gazed out the window. The cruise ship was long gone, but a Manly ferry was approaching Circular Quay, leaving white frothy water in its wake.

As much as he loved his siblings, he also loved his peace and quiet. He sometimes wondered about their grandfather and whether he'd be pleased with how his grandchildren were handling his fortune. James Barrington was renowned for his kindness, a rarity in the ruthless mining industry, and Nicholas wished he'd gotten to know him better before he passed. He sensed he could have learned a lot from him, and not just about the business. He'd heard that James Barrington was a religious man. Another rarity in the industry.

Swivelling his chair all the way around, Nicholas set back to work, tapping his fingers on the keyboard, opening emails from clients, studying spreadsheets. Millions of dollars in transactions and exchanges occurred on a weekly basis and the company was doing well, but as Managing Director, he needed to stay on top of it.

Their clients were happy, and he had reason to be proud of the company that he and his siblings had maintained and grown since taking over almost ten years ago. To the world at large, they were a success.

But sometimes, in the still of night, when he had time to think, he pondered what success really was. What was he missing by spending all his days on the forty-fifth floor?

CHAPTER 2

Making her way to the teacher's lounge, Phoebe Halliday smiled and greeted all those she passed. No matter how she felt inside, no matter what thoughts passed through her mind each day, she outwardly remained positive, energised, and grateful. Nobody wanted to see a sad face.

She sat at the table she usually shared with her friend, Johanna, the other kindergarten teacher who also doubled as the music teacher. People often confused the two since they both had similar medium-brown hair and light eyes, although Phoebe's were more of a grey-blue than Johanna's hazel ones.

Opening her bag, she pulled out a plastic container filled with leftovers from the previous night's dinner. Sensing someone approaching, she glanced up and was surprised to see Mrs. Jamison, the school counsellor, and not Johanna, hovering beside the table.

Mrs. Jamison, friendly and grey-haired, was always on the

lookout for someone in need of care. Although she had great respect for the woman, Phoebe groaned inwardly. She didn't want to be the subject of her caring attention right now.

"Hi, Phoebe." Mrs. Jamison smiled. "Do you mind if I sit here?"

Phoebe returned her smile. Despite how she was feeling, she couldn't be rude. "Not at all. Please feel free."

As Mrs. Jamison sat next to her, Phoebe sensed that this might be more than just a friendly visit.

"I'm taking an early lunch because I'm watching my grandson's football game this afternoon," Mrs. Jamison explained, unwrapping her chicken and salad sandwich.

"Oh, that sounds nice." Phoebe opened her lunch box and wished she'd made a sandwich instead of bringing leftover pasta.

"Yes. I don't get to watch often." Pausing, she turned and faced Phoebe. "So, how are you doing?"

Phoebe winced. This was the exact question she'd been dreading. It was the last thing she wanted to discuss, and Mrs. Jamison would be very aware of that. "Oh, you know," she replied with a fake smile as she twiddled her fork.

"I may know a lot about human behaviour, Phoebe, but that doesn't mean I know what's going on inside your head." Her eyes were filled with kindness. "If you ever need to talk to anyone, you know I'm here, don't you?" Mrs. Jamison patted her arm lightly.

Suddenly losing her appetite, Phoebe set her fork down and stared at her nails. Could she tell Mrs. Jamison what she was really thinking or feeling? Could she tell her about the grief that still weighed her down daily? Would she understand?

Phoebe wasn't the first person to lose a fiancé, but that didn't make handling it any easier. It didn't stop her from feeling alone. It didn't stop her from wondering why God had allowed her to lose Reed, just weeks before their wedding. She tried so hard to trust Him, and she knew that God loved her, but nevertheless, she struggled to understand. "Thank you," she replied softly. "It's been hard to find anyone to talk with who really understands."

Mrs. Jamison nodded, her eyes full of compassion. Most people didn't know what to say, and simply offered their condolences, but they had no idea of the extent of the grief she still felt. Phoebe didn't blame them. How could they know if they hadn't lost someone special?

She took a deep breath. "Trying to explain how I felt after Reed passed away has seemed impossible, as if all of the words I had died with him."

"Grief does that sometimes," Mrs. Jamison said. "It's easier to keep it bottled than try to explain it."

"Yes," Phoebe replied. "I don't think I've truly accepted that Reed will never be my husband. All those years of loving him and planning our future together, they mean nothing anymore." Tears welled in her eyes.

"It takes time, Phoebe, and it's okay to grieve. But it's also good to talk about it," Mrs. Jamison said softly, passing her a tissue.

Phoebe nodded and dabbed her eyes. "I don't know what I'm mourning most. The Reed I miss, or the Reed Fisher I dreamed of as my husband. We should have been married by now."

"I understand. It seems that all of your dreams died with him."

Phoebe nodded. That was exactly it.

"But I'm proud of you, Phoebe. The way you've handled yourself has been an example to all. But you don't need to pretend you're strong if you're not. It really is okay to show that you're grieving. People will understand."

Phoebe smiled weakly as memories of that day flooded back, three weeks before their wedding, when she got the phone call that changed her life. She recalled the dread that filled her when she heard that Reed was in critical condition. She couldn't believe it was him. They'd gotten it wrong and it was someone else. It couldn't be him.

But it was. And he didn't make it. Her fiancé, the one she'd planned to spend the rest of her life with, was dead.

She burst into tears as the all familiar ache tore through her heart once again. Mrs. Jamison shifted closer and embraced her while she wept against the older woman's chest.

After she calmed, Mrs. Jamison suggested she take the rest of the day off, but Phoebe said no, she was fine. It was better to be at school with her class of five-year-olds than to be at home, moping.

"That's exactly the attitude I was talking about, Phoebe. You're doing so well, but if you need time off, make sure you take it. Okay?"

Phoebe nodded, but doubted she would.

She'd made plans to meet up with her closest friend, Holly Mathison, later that afternoon. After the emotionally draining day, she was tempted to cancel, but in the end, decided to go.

Arriving first at *Aroma*, their favourite coffee shop, she

chose a booth. Holly arrived a few minutes late, which didn't surprise Phoebe at all since Holly was always late for everything. Phoebe raised her hand and waved her over, standing to give her friend a hug.

Tall and curvy with fair skin, blue eyes and straight sandy hair, Holly was Phoebe's complete opposite. Being petite, Phoebe had to stretch up on her toes to hug her friend.

"Sorry I'm late," Holly said, wincing as she slid into the booth opposite Phoebe.

Phoebe tried not to laugh. "You mean this time, right?"

"Yeah, okay, I know. I'm always late. Funny," Holly replied with sarcasm.

"True, but I love you anyway."

"Good! How are those chicks of yours doing?

Phoebe chuckled as she sipped her water. Every year she borrowed eggs from a local farmer and brought them into her classroom. She set them under a heat lamp, and her class of five-year-olds watched and waited eagerly for the little chicks to hatch. "They're doing great. Come and see them before I send them back to the farmer."

Holly smiled. "I might just do that."

The waitress delivered the coffees Phoebe had ordered when she arrived. Holly stirred a sachet of sugar into hers, and then, wrapping her hands around the mug, put her elbows on the table and leaned forward. "So, remember what I was saying about having the travel bug?"

"Yep. I seem to recall you told me that it's the only infection you'd ever volunteer for," Phoebe replied with a laugh.

"Exactly. I've been thinking through a few things." Pausing,

Holly sipped her coffee. "Let me tell you my thoughts, then let me pose a question."

Phoebe tilted her head. This wasn't the sort of conversation they typically had.

"So," Holly continued, "I'm planning to go travelling for three months, and I finally decided, due to finances and proximity, to do a backpacking trip in Southeast Asia."

"That sounds wonderful." Phoebe smiled as she imagined her adventurous friend travelling through the countryside, seeing amazing sights, riding elephants, visiting temples.

"Yeah, it's going to be amazing. I've already looked into the details and requirements of visas and shots. I'll start in Cambodia and stay until I feel like moving on to the next place. There are some amazing organisations to volunteer at as well. I'll be going as a tourist, but I've already contacted a few places about volunteering for a few days or even a week, just helping wherever I can."

"That sounds great." Phoebe tried not to sound jealous.

"Yeah. I've already had one orphanage say they're inundated with volunteers, and it breaks the kids' hearts whenever they leave. I don't want to be a part of that, but another place has invited me to do a three-day English tutorial with some of the older kids they work with," Holly continued.

"Seriously? That's great. Is it an orphanage as well?" Phoebe asked.

Holly shook her head. "No. They're mainly girls who've been rescued from brothels they were trafficked into."

"Oh, gosh." Phoebe's hand flew to her mouth. She knew these things happened, but the thought of it was too horrific to imagine.

"I know. And that leads me to my question." Pausing, Holly twiddled a lock of hair and held Phoebe's gaze.

"Yes…" Somehow, she knew what Holly was about to ask and her heartbeat quickened.

"You've had a rough year, Phoebe. You've suffered pain and trauma—"

"Yes, but nothing like what those girls have gone through," Phoebe interjected, unable to move her thoughts past what she'd just heard.

"Maybe, but that doesn't lessen your pain." Holly gripped her hand. "You've been making such an effort to be brave and to get through your suffering, but Phoebe, you need time away."

Phoebe knew exactly where Holly was going, and she didn't take much convincing. Both Mrs. Jamison and Holly were right. She needed some time off. Drawing a steadying breath, she held Holly's gaze. "I'm in. When do we leave?"

Holly's eyes widened. "Just like that? My practical friend is willing to make a spontaneous decision?"

Phoebe smiled. "I'm more than willing. I'm raring to go. When do we leave?"

CHAPTER 3

From the moment he laid eyes on Kailey, the woman his brother had recommended he take to dinner, Nicholas knew she wasn't his type, despite Alden assuring him they had much in common.

After arriving at the restaurant and being shown to a table, he made the mistake of complimenting her dress. He didn't know what else to say, and as soon as the words flowed from his mouth, he wished he could take them back. The story that followed was a run-on sentence about the fact that she'd purchased a different dress the day before. Apparently, after trying it on again at home, she didn't feel it highlighted an ample part of her body that she clearly took pride in. Well, this outfit certainly did. Nicholas made every effort to not be completely distracted by the dress that showed off her favourite feature very well. For a first date, it didn't make the right impression at all. Well, not for him, at least.

Maybe she was just nervous. He'd give her the benefit of

the doubt, but if first impressions were anything to go by, there wouldn't be a second date.

"So, I don't know. I guess I just didn't like it that much. You know what I mean?" Leaning forward, she revealed even more of her ample features while sipping her wine.

Nicholas nodded, planting a fake smile on his face. "Y-yeah, I get what you mean. I have trouble finding dresses all the time." He hoped a joke might distract her. It didn't work. She tilted her head like she was confused. Maybe she thought he was some sort of freak who liked to wear women's clothing. Jokes obviously weren't going to work.

He gestured for the waiter. They already had their wine, but it was time to order and he'd been subtly perusing the menu during the previous conversation. "You order first," he said with his smile still firmly planted.

"Thank you." His date looked up at the waiter and batted her long eyelashes. "What's the duck comfort? It's really expensive, so I'm guessing it's good?"

Nicholas managed to keep a straight face while the waiter smiled politely. "*Oui, Madame.* The duck confit is one of our best dishes. *C'est très bien.*"

Nicholas had chosen this restaurant not only because they served authentic French cuisine, but it was owned and run by a family who'd emigrated from France and they were passionate about their food and culture. The fact that the dinner was likely to cost him an arm and a leg was moot point until he actually met Kailey. Now he knew the dinner would likely be wasted on her.

"So, what do you enjoy doing?" he asked once they'd placed their orders.

She took a large sip of wine. "Hmmm… let me see." Pausing, she adjusted the straps on her dress. Nick averted his gaze. "I like to watch football."

"Really?" Interest piqued, he turned his head and faced her. "I love football. I play occasionally, but I don't know many women who enjoy it."

Her eyes lit up. "I started watching when my ex was playing. I could barely take my eyes off all those hunky guys."

Nicholas groaned inwardly. So much for thinking they might share an interest. But maybe they had other things in common. "What about reading?" he asked, suggesting another pastime he enjoyed.

"Oh, I love to read!" she exclaimed, her eyes widening. "There's a new local author who's especially good. Helen something or other. She writes modern romance about witches in Sydney. It's so entertaining!"

Again, Nicholas was left disappointed. He hadn't expected Kailey to be his perfect match, but everything she said confirmed they weren't suited at all. He let her talk, which she had no trouble doing, but he wasn't listening. He was relieved when the waiter finally arrived with their meals.

"Right. Well here's the food." He rubbed his hands together after nodding his thanks to the waiter.

"Finally." She blew out a breath as she picked up her silverware. "Maybe next time we can go somewhere that has faster service."

Nicholas shook his head. Was she for real? After taking a few mouthfuls of his *bœuf bourguignon*, he asked her how the duck was.

"Um…it's okay I guess. I don't know, I just thought it would be more chicken-y."

"You mean, the duck doesn't taste like the chicken that cost half the price?" He tilted his head in mock surprise.

"I know, right? I'm thinking that maybe they don't even use real duck." She lowered her voice, as if it were a conspiracy.

He ate a few more mouthfuls and then dabbed his mouth with a napkin. He couldn't prolong the agony any longer. "You know, Kailey, I have to be honest. We're very different, and I don't think this is working."

"You noticed it, too? We have really different energies," she replied, flipping her hair over her shoulder.

"Exactly," Nicholas said, deciding to simply go with her explanation.

"So, like, what do you think we should do?"

"I think we should go our separate ways. I'll head home, if you don't mind, but you're welcome to stay if you like. Or I can organize a lift for you."

"Right. So you're dumping me?" She raised a finely plucked brow.

Nicholas bit his lip. He hadn't meant it to come out that way. "I don't know if I'd call it that. It was only a first date, after all, but I don't think we should do it again." He gave an apologetic smile.

"Okay then, sure. I'll finish this fake duck and you can run off," she replied offhandedly, swirling her wine glass.

He had no idea if he ought to interpret her response as offense or relief, but after offering another apology and bidding a polite goodbye, he asked the waiter to charge his card and to package up his meal while he waited outside. It was an awkward exit, but he didn't want to waste the food.

Finally pulling out of the car park, Nicholas breathed a sigh of relief as he headed his car towards his home. The date had been a disaster. He'd been out with shallow girls before, but Kailey certainly took the cake for being the worst. He had no idea why Alden thought they had anything in common.

Fifteen minutes from his home, he passed by the church he'd been attending. He'd gone to the mid-week service a few nights before, but was surprised to see the car park almost full on a Saturday evening. He wasn't aware anything was on.

With nothing to lose, he turned into the car park and found a spot. He glanced at his dinner which the waiter had placed in an insulated bag and hoped it would keep until later. Either way, he was interested in what might be going on inside.

Not wanting to be recognised as 'that rich guy', he slipped a pair of glasses on and removed his tie. He had no idea if his attempts to disguise his identity worked or not, but so far it seemed he'd flown under the radar, although he normally slipped in the back and sat by himself, and then slipped out again before the service ended. Maybe it worked, maybe it didn't.

A table had been set up in the foyer and was hosted by two young women he hadn't seen before. He wouldn't be able to slip in unseen tonight.

"Hi!" one of the girls greeted enthusiastically. "Do you have a ticket or do you want to buy one?"

Nicholas scratched his head. "Well, first I'm curious about what's going on. I wasn't aware there were any events on Saturdays."

"Oh, it's great! Tonight we have two of our missionaries from Thailand speaking. They're hosting a benefit dinner for their organisation, 'Regenerate the Nations'," the girl explained.

"That sounds interesting. What kind of organisation is it?"

"They rescue and rehabilitate victims of sex trafficking. It's an amazing centre. I went earlier this year on a mission trip, and it was awesome. The dinner started about ten minutes ago, but I think you've made it in time for the presentation."

"Perfect. I'll take a ticket, thanks." Nicholas felt a sudden urge to do something out of the ordinary. He could eat his fancy French dinner tomorrow. Tonight, he'd have a dinner that fed his soul.

After buying a ticket, he walked hesitantly into the fellowship hall. It was filled with tables. Most were taken, but he found one towards the back with a spare seat. After confirming it wasn't reserved, he sat on the plastic chair and pulled up to the table. It wasn't long before the waiter, a volunteer he recognised from the worship team, brought him a plate of Pad Thai that smelled wonderful.

The couple beside him introduced themselves as Bill and Norma. After introducing himself as Nick, he engaged in polite conversation with them. They told him that while they were too old to travel, they'd been blessed financially and supported the organisation because they believed in what they were doing. Nicholas nodded respectfully.

After only a few moments of interaction, the speaker, a shortish man Nicholas guessed might be in his mid-thirties, moved to the stage and adjusted the microphone. A slide on the screen behind him displayed an image of Bangkok at night —a vibrant city, filled with colour and light.

"Good evening, everyone. Thank you all for coming. My name is Thomas Edwards. Many of you know me, but for those who don't, I and my lovely wife, Judy," pausing, he gestured to a woman seated near the front who raised her hand, "are missionaries in Bangkok, Thailand.

"We moved there eight years ago after spending three years in training. In those three years, we visited Thailand several times and worked in a number of mission organisations. By the time we moved there, we were certain that the Lord had called us to work in serving the young women who'd been trafficked through numerous brothels in the city of Bangkok.

"With the help of this church and the rest of our partners, we were able to set up this facility you can see on the screen." He clicked to the next slide. "This shot was taken on the day we purchased it. As you can see, it was quite run down, but now, after a lot of TLC, it looks like this." He clicked again and soft gasps moved around the room. The difference was truly amazing. They'd done a great job improving the run-down building and now it looked attractive with fresh paint, a small garden at the front filled with colourful flowers, and a sign hanging over the doorway that Nicholas couldn't read, but assumed said 'welcome'. It looked like a place young girls might feel safe coming to.

"This is where we run our day centre," Thomas continued. "Upstairs we have housing for emergency placements. Our day centre is where we run our prevention and rehabilitation programs and where we try to help victims of sex trafficking overcome their pasts and give them hope for a better future. We also teach parents and children to be aware of the dangers that are all around them, and how easy it is for the unwary to

21

get entrapped in the sex industry. Prevention is always better than cure."

The photos of young, innocent faces flicked across the screen, some so young, it broke Nicholas's heart. It was too much. He couldn't sit by and watch any longer. He knew then what he'd do. He'd not just give money, he'd volunteer. He could definitely use a break from both work and family, and it was more than time he did something more meaningful than sit in a fancy office playing with figures.

CHAPTER 4

*D*isembarking the plane at Phnom Penh International Airport, Phoebe stepped into a wall of suffocating heat. She was used to warm temperatures, but this was different; it was so thick she could almost hold the air in her hand. But she and Holly were finally here in Cambodia, about to start their adventure, so she shrugged the discomfort off. They'd get used to it, along with everything else.

Having never been to an Asian country before, they were both excited about experiencing new things, and as they joined the line to pass through customs and immigration, Phoebe gazed around her, watching and listening. So many different languages, and the outfits were so vibrant and colourful. It was a feast for her senses and the buzz was contagious.

The line took less time than they'd anticipated, and once they had their passports stamped and visas confirmed, they found their way through the crowd to the outside of the airport where they lined up for a taxi to take them to their hotel. The line moved quickly and soon they were seated in the back of an old taxi with a driver who spoke little English.

Phoebe tried to take it all in, but there was so much to see. The traffic was unbelievable. Cars, trucks, bicycles, three-wheeled *tuk-tuks*, and motorbikes carrying everything from huge boxes to entire families, all jostling for space on the busy road.

Finally, the driver pulled over and stopped. The girls looked up at the building and then at each other. "Is this it?" Holly pulled her itinerary out and glanced at it.

"I think so," Phoebe replied. It was smaller than it looked in the photos, but she knew that a lot of hotels used that marketing ploy. Flattering photos attracted customers.

They paid the driver and carried their bags inside. After checking in and settling into their shared room, they found that even though the hotel didn't quite live up to their expectations, it wasn't so bad. It had two single beds which were neatly made up, a bench with a kettle, two mugs and tea and coffee sachets, a small television in the corner, and a tiny balcony overlooking the busy road. Most importantly of all, it had air-conditioning.

Collapsing onto her bed, Phoebe placed a hand against her sweaty forehead. "I think I'll be staying inside for a while to cool off."

"Come on, Phoebes. It's not that hot. We're in Cambodia. We can't stay in our hotel all day," Holly said, gazing through the glass door to the street below.

Phoebe sat up. "You're right. I'll take a shower and then I'll feel better."

Holly turned around and smiled. "Good plan. Um, what's

this?" She stared at the piece of paper she'd just picked up from beside the television.

"What?" Puzzled, Phoebe stood and moved closer to see what Holly was looking at. "Oh my goodness!" Her hand flew to her mouth. It was an advertisement, on hotel letterhead, for a local brothel offering girls for any customers who wanted them. A variety of ages and price points were available, and discretion was guaranteed.

"We need to stay somewhere else," Holly said, tossing the paper aside like it was poison. She quickly grabbed her bag. "I don't know how we made such a huge mistake."

"I don't know either." Phoebe grabbed her bag, too, stuffing the items she'd already unpacked back into it.

"All the reviews were good," Holly added.

"We know how they can be skewed." Phoebe zipped her bag up and then ran her hand across her limp hair. "What are we going to do, Holl? We thought this hotel was going to be all right. How do we know they're not all the same?"

Holly flopped onto a chair. "You're right. We need to think this through."

"Maybe we should pray about it," Phoebe suggested quietly.

"Good idea. Let's do that," Holly replied.

The girls bowed their heads. Phoebe took a deep breath to still her heart before she began. "Lord, we're very aware that we're in a foreign country, but we need somewhere safer to stay. We don't feel comfortable staying in a place where sin is so blatantly encouraged. Please help us find somewhere more suitable."

Holly also prayed, and after they finished with a quiet 'Amen', she suggested they make a list of nearby hotels.

"Maybe we should call the place where we're volunteering. They might have some recommendations," Phoebe suggested.

"Another good idea, Phoebes. We should have done that in the first place." Holly sounded despondent.

"We didn't know, Holl. It's okay. We'll find somewhere."

Holly gave a grateful smile. "You're right. I'll give them a call."

Phoebe listened to Holly's side of the conversation, stifling giggles as her friend tried to make herself understood. When she got off the phone, Holly relayed to Phoebe that the woman at the organisation had agreed to send their driver to pick them up and deliver them to a better hotel.

Phoebe smiled. "That's great, Holl. You did well."

"Thanks. I just wish I knew more of the language."

"You know more than me!" Phoebe said, heading to the door.

Holly laughed. "That wouldn't be hard." Having studied Asian languages at university, Holly was reasonably fluent in Vietnamese and Chinese and muddled through with Kmer and Thai, which Phoebe was very glad about.

Phoebe let her speak with the woman at the front desk when they returned downstairs to check out, offering support by standing beside her and nodding when she thought it appropriate. Holly stood a good head and shoulders above the short-haired, middle-aged Cambodian woman, but she didn't seem intimidated by Holly's height. At one stage, Phoebe thought it might end in an argument, but Holly remained calm and the woman finally agreed to refund them all but one night's tariff. "You won't find any better," she called after the girls as they headed for the door.

26

Holly turned and smiled. "We'll see."

They waited outside for almost half an hour and were growing anxious by the time the driver arrived, especially as daylight was fast fading. Bunroeun was a sweet, older man who quickly loaded their luggage into his car. "We get you to better place. This place not good," he said in broken English.

"Thank you so much for coming for us. We're very tired," Phoebe replied.

"You have been travelling all day?" He looked in the rear vision mirror as he drove, a perpetual smile on his sun-beaten, friendly face.

The girls nodded.

As they drove along the streets, Phoebe looked out the window and realised with dismay that many of the young women weren't just girls going out in the evening as she and Holly did back home. They were looking for customers, and possibly also recruiting for their brothels.

"Why do so many girls get caught up in trafficking, Bunroeun? There seem to be so many of them."

Turning his head slightly, his jaw tightened. "Many families rely on their daughter to support them with money they earn. And oftentimes, the mistress buy girl with promise of more, or they tell girl and her family from other country that they will become rich here with good job."

While his voice remained even and factual, Phoebe had no doubt that it broke his heart to see the children of his country exploited in such a way.

"Many girl are told that if they bring new girl, their time will be less. They can go home to their family sooner. So they bring new girl. The house mistress very clever," he added.

"That's terrible," Holly said, sounding grieved and a little angry.

"Yes, very terrible," Bunroeun agreed.

They reached a hotel that from the outside looked much nicer than the previous one. At least the paint wasn't falling off, but appearances could be deceptive. Bunroeun assured them that the price was comparable and the owner was one of the men working with their organisation to fight against the local trafficking. "You will be looked after here. No worries." Although his smile was genuine, a horrid thought ran through Phoebe's mind. *What if he was part of the racket?* She pushed the thought away. They had to trust someone, and they'd prayed about it. Surely he was on the level.

Her concerns were forgotten when the manager greeted them warmly and showed them to their room, which was larger and far nicer than their previous one, making Phoebe wonder if they'd been upgraded.

After unpacking and showering, she settled in for the night and fell asleep immediately. She dreamed of waking in the morning and being surrounded by Cambodian children like the ones in her kindergarten class, but instead, she woke to a horrible itch around her left eye. She immediately thought of bed bugs, but when she looked in the mirror and saw it was just a little puffy and red, she figured she'd had some sort of allergic reaction to the pillow and vowed to wrap it in a T-shirt for the rest of their time there.

"Put this against it," Holly instructed, handing Phoebe a small bag of ice cubes she'd found in the freezer.

"Thanks." It felt instantly better, and by the time they were ready to go down for breakfast, the puffiness had all but disappeared.

"So, Bunroeun is picking us up again and will drive us to the complex for our English classes. I've been assigned a fourteen to sixteen-year old class, and you'll be with the eight to ten-year-old class," Holly reminded Phoebe.

"I can't wait to meet them," Phoebe said.

"Neither can I, but it's going to be challenging. We'll have a training session first because so many of these kids have been traumatised, and they want to be sure we won't do or say anything to trigger any memories and such like. We have to be careful with how we interact with them."

"But my students are so young."

"Phoebe, your students aren't from the prevention centre. They're from the rescue centre, just like mine."

Phoebe couldn't have been more gob-smacked. How had she missed that? Why had she assumed that because the children she'd been assigned were so young that they hadn't been abused? They were eight to ten-year-olds. Little children. Mostly girls, but also a few boys, and they'd already suffered such horrific things.

"Sorry, I thought I told you that we're both in the rescue department while we're here," Holly apologised.

"Somehow I missed that bit of information."

The day seemed to be a whirlwind of activity from there. Bunroeun collected them and drove them to the centre. It was called 'Hesed', a Hebrew word reflecting the loyal love people committed to God should have for one another. After their initial briefing with Donovan, 'Hesed's' director, Phoebe met her class of twenty students.

The little faces broke her heart when she thought about the terrible things they'd experienced. So many children and so much hurt and heartache. She made every effort to make the class fun, allowing them to make up stories in broken English, sing English songs, dance together. She had so much fun with them that for a while she forgot about the tragedies they'd suffered in the past.

But would a few English classes help them to forget? Would the children ever be able to move on from the horrors they'd experienced? It could take a lifetime to heal, but like her with her grief over losing Reed, it was a process, and every step forward would help.

AFTER THE THREE days of English classes, the girls were assigned other odd jobs around the complex. They also learned about outreach to the pimps, where these men and women who were responsible for ruining so many young lives were encouraged to leave their lives of trafficking and abuse behind and open their hearts to God.

The girls were impressed that anyone who needed assistance was welcomed into the centre. No one was excluded, and the centre was doing a great job, but after two weeks, they started to discuss where they should go next. They'd set aside three months for their travels, and it was becoming clear that although they felt welcome at 'Hesed', the centre didn't need them. Teaching the English classes had been a great experience, but there were regular teachers who could teach the students. They agreed it was time to move on.

Phoebe took a sip of water as they sat at a table in the local café they'd been frequenting, waiting for their meals to arrive. "This experience has been amazing, and if we want to continue volunteering, Thailand has several places we can go."

"The ones Donovan mentioned?" Holly asked.

"No, these are ones I know about from church. There's one we support, along with a few other churches around Sydney. 'Regenerate the Nations'. It sounds like an amazing place, a lot like this one, and we'd probably get assigned some classes there. I can send an email and ask," Phoebe suggested.

"Sounds good." Holly smiled and then thanked the waitress when their meals were delivered.

Within two hours after sending her email, Phoebe received a reply saying they'd be more than welcome, and she and Holly immediately set about making their travel arrangements to fly to Bangkok.

Bunroeun was sad when he heard they were leaving and invited them for dinner at his house the night before their departure. "You going to be missed," he assured them. His wife didn't speak any English, but smiled delightfully all evening. Phoebe felt certain she'd never seen such joy in a woman.

As she witnessed the love Bunroeun and his wife shared, she felt a fresh twinge of pain in her heart. She'd done well so far on the trip. Helping others had certainly helped take her mind off her own troubles and sadness, but seeing this loving couple together brought everything back.

Reed was gone and she knew it, but with God's help, she *was* starting to move forward, and she had hope that by serving others who'd suffered more than she could ever imagine, her own grief would lessen.

CHAPTER 5

"Oh, nice! A vacation in Thailand?" Alden echoed. "Great choice. Beautiful women, great city life. I didn't know you had it in you to do something like that, big brother." Alden slapped Nicholas on the back, a roguish grin on his face.

"Well, you know, I just need a bit of time off." Nicholas had no desire to tell his brother and sister exactly what he was planning for his time in Thailand, but he knew it was good timing. Charity was returning from Bali in a few days, and a week later, he'd take off for Thailand to volunteer with 'Regenerate the Nations'.

The night of the benefit dinner, Thomas had stated that they were low on staff because they didn't have enough financial support to hire as many full-time workers as they needed. Too many of their employees, believing in the good of the work, were covering multiple positions and working longer hours than they should.

Arriving home, Nicholas signed up on their website to be a regular donor. While he made a generous donation, he refrained from making it too generous before he'd seen the work for himself and could satisfy himself that the money was indeed going to where they claimed.

Several of his senior staffers hinted subtly that taking a whole month off from work when they were so busy was a little crazy. Nevertheless, they were excited for him, knowing that he worked hard and deserved a break. If Charity and Alden could take time off, as they often did, he should be able to as well. That reasoning was working well in his favour and he was thankful that most people thought that way.

But he was concerned. Other people from Sydney would be working at the mission, like Thomas and Judy, and possibly more. He didn't want to be known as the billionaire taking a few weeks off to do something philanthropic to make himself feel better. This wasn't the first charitable cause he'd cared about and given to consistently, but this was different. It would be the first one he'd personally be visiting and actually working at.

After he made the announcement, he could hardly walk down the hall without someone making a comment about how jealous they were or what a good idea it was for him to take a break. He was beginning to feel frustrated, but he tried to ignore it. No one knew his real reason for going. They thought he was going for the girls, the night-life, and the shopping. He couldn't blame them for that. It was his own choice to keep his real reason quiet.

But he needed a way to keep his identity hidden. A beard, perhaps? Thinking it might help, he stopped shaving a week ahead of his flight, and as expected, received relentless teasing from his siblings and a few colleagues, but most thought it looked decent on him.

He decided also to shorten his name to Nick, like he'd done at church that night. He could do little about his surname, but he hoped that wouldn't pop up too often, if at all.

The week before he was to leave was spent busily preparing. But as he bought toys to give to the children and packed them in his bag, he began wondering what he would be doing there.

"Oh, you know, just touristy stuff," Nicholas answered his sister when she asked him the same question after returning from her trip and hearing about his.

Being evasive was easy, but picturing the reality was much more difficult. Would he be assigned cleaning duties? Raiding brothels? Perhaps teaching students in a computer class?

"Well, don't be an obnoxious tourist. You know, I met so many of those on my journey and I can hardly tell you what boorish people Australians, Brits, and Americans can be when travelling around Southeast Asia," Charity had said.

Nicholas held his tongue so he wouldn't accidentally tell her that she was one of those obnoxious people. "Well, I'm glad you understood how to be respectful at least," he encouraged.

"Oh, of course. I mean, going to the meditation centre was amazing. The people there just love to serve! They were so attentive and I was glad to give them a chance to do what they enjoy," she told him ignorantly.

Nicholas thought how sad that the Balinese had to deal with so many ignorant western women who knew nothing of their culture but were more than happy to exploit them.

Women who didn't follow their religion, but enjoyed its trendy appeal. He couldn't imagine that any of the Balinese really felt honoured to be able to serve them as Charity seemed to believe. Maybe they did, but it was more likely that they were simply doing what they needed to do to earn money to support their families.

He wasn't willing to be the one to point that out to Charity. She could live in her naiveté, but he hoped that someday she'd change and become a more tolerant and empathetic individual. For now, it seemed that Charity and Alden considered themselves entitled and that the world revolved around them.

They had lunch together again on the last day before he left.

"See? Even you won't fly with our pilot. As usual. And yet you forbid us from firing him? What a hypocrite," Charity mumbled.

"You know I never use the jet, but that doesn't mean I have anything against Roger. He's the best there is. So no, I'm not going to let you fire him for things that aren't his fault," Nicholas repeated. Again.

"Then why don't you take the jet?" Alden challenged.

Nicholas sighed. He could hardly try to explain it to them now. "I just don't think it's necessary. You know I never have. I've always believed in going through traditional travel arrangements and boarding a plane like everyone else. I don't need special treatment."

"That's a poor excuse for saying you don't like the man's flight skills," Alden joked under his breath.

Nicholas raked a hand through his hair. He couldn't explain it, so there was little point in making the effort to try. And if he did take the jet simply to prove his support of Roger, he knew too well that taking it *would* be the thing that made a hypocrite of him. How could he justifiably fly in a private jet when he was going to the mission as a volunteer? There was no way he could do that, even if he wanted to.

That night, Nicholas went through his suitcases a final time, checking to ensure everything was in order. Once confident it was, he carried his bags to the garage and loaded them into his sleek, black Porsche. Closing the boot, he nodded in satisfaction. Tomorrow, everything would change for him. He could feel it. This trip was going to be the experience of a lifetime.

CHAPTER 6

"*Y*ou're doing such a great job!" Phoebe declared to Sukhonn, a small dark-haired girl in her assigned class.

Much like 'Hesed', 'Regenerate the Nations' took a holistic approach towards dealing with trafficking. As well as the rehabilitation programs, they also ran prevention programs, like the one Phoebe was now working in with children of a similar age to those she taught back home.

The children were mostly from poor and vulnerable families who couldn't afford school, so classes were offered for free if they couldn't pay the small fee.

As before, Holly worked in the rehabilitation department with older students who'd previously been victims of trafficking. Phoebe admired Holly's devotion to these young women who'd been so traumatised and were often difficult to work with as a result.

There was also a class for males who'd been trafficked, but

it was held at a sister campus nearby. 'Regenerate the Nations' had seen the need for offering a separate option for boys, and while staff were intermixed in order to give survivors an opportunity to interact with both men and women, they worked hard to ensure all the children felt comfortable, especially when dealing with the opposite sex.

The outreach program to the pimps was one of the most incredible initiatives Phoebe had ever seen. At the same time as staff from 'Regenerate the Nations' held raids to rescue the children, a specially trained team also tried to reach the pimps. When any were arrested, the team visited them in prison, playing football and other games with them to befriend them and gain their trust. They sought to be positive influences in the pimps' lives, and encouraged them not to return to pimping when they were released from prison, but to seek different lines of work. Opportunities were made available for them to learn new skills so they had options.

They weren't all success stories, but enough men left the lucrative sex business and chose a better path because of the team's input, spurring the team on to continue this work.

All of that aside, Phoebe was simply thankful for the little ones she had the opportunity to work with during her time at the mission. Occasionally she wondered if God was calling her to live there permanently and serve full-time. She wasn't sure, but if not, she could support the mission financially and help fund more teachers. It saddened her that the classes were so large, and that the kindergarten aged students were usually with the first and second graders since there was only one woman to teach them all. For an organisation doing such good work, it wasn't right that they struggled for support.

"Hey!" Holly poked her head inside Phoebe's classroom, an impish grin on her face.

"Hey," Phoebe greeted and waved her in.

"Did you see the new volunteer?" Holly whispered in her ear.

Phoebe shook her head. "No. I think I heard Thomas say someone was coming, but that was a few days ago and I totally forgot."

"You should meet him." Holly winked.

Phoebe knew that wink. It was Holly's way of acknowledging the man was attractive. "Oh, right, as in, you want to meet him?" she teased in reply.

"I don't know. He's cute, but you know I have my eye on someone back home."

"Well, since you've chosen to be away for three months, I don't think you're overly interested in that guy back home," Phoebe pointed out.

Holly shrugged. "Whatever. My point is, *you* ought to meet this guy. He's one handsome dude." With that, she stepped into the corridor and proceeded on her way.

Shaking her head, Phoebe immediately dismissed Holly's suggestion. She'd come away to heal from her loss. To learn to live with her grief. What made Holly think she'd have any interest in a shallow vacation romance? She returned her attention to her class. "Okay, time to clean up," she said, forgetting all about Holly and the new volunteer. There was another lesson to get through before lunch.

When lunch finally came around, she went to the staff dining room and joined Holly who was already seated. "How was your last class?" Phoebe asked as she inspected her noodle meal.

"Good. Yours?" Holly replied before taking a mouthful of her Pad Thai.

"Good. But not as good as this food. Why didn't we come to Thailand sooner?" Phoebe picked up her chop sticks and began to dig into the meal.

Her seat faced the door, and when an unfamiliar man walked in, she momentarily stopped chewing, assuming he was the guy Holly had mentioned. With dark, wavy hair, a stubble of a beard, and a mischievous glint in his striking blue eyes, she was right. He was downright handsome. Phoebe didn't realise she'd been staring until Holly waved a hand in front of her face. "Hello…"

"Oh, sorry," Phoebe said, startled and embarrassed. She looked down at her meal and continued chewing.

Holly turned in the man's direction and then back at Phoebe, raising a brow. "Told you," she whispered under her breath.

"So you did. But it doesn't matter. He's handsome, but the last thing I want right now is to get side-tracked by anyone. The distraction won't do me any good," Phoebe reminded her friend.

"No, but there's no harm in being friendly."

Phoebe shrugged. "You're right, but I'm here to heal from my loss. Well, that was my initial reason for coming. That's changed a little now, and I'm glad to be here, helping wherever I can."

Holly studied her for a moment. "Okay then, I won't push."

"Thank you." Phoebe smiled appreciatively, and yet, she

couldn't help stealing another glance at the handsome stranger who was smiling warmly at the Thai woman handing him his meal.

She hoped Holly wouldn't wave him over, and was relieved when she didn't and he sat at a table on his own. Maybe they should have offered for him to join them, it almost seemed rude not to, but he didn't seem the sort of man who was seeking attention. In fact, she sensed he was trying hard not to be noticed. Although, with his looks, that would be impossible. She liked the fact that a good-looking man could seem so humble. Humble *and* gracious.

"So, tell me more about the kids in your class. You said you have a little girl who was really struggling last week. Has she improved at all?" Holly asked.

"A little. She allowed me to read to her, and that in itself was a step forward. Before, she was hardly willing to even enter the classroom. She doesn't trust anyone and doesn't want to be with people."

"Do you think she's experienced trauma?" Holly asked quietly.

Phoebe nodded. "I think so. It's the most likely explanation. But I'm doing my best to be cautious so I don't startle her. I've set aside the back corner for any child who might need some alone time. So many of them have been through terrible experiences from what I gather."

"And that's the prevention class," Holly asked, although it was more a statement.

"Exactly. It's so sad, but it's great that there are places like this that are trying to take care of the children and their families, and even reaching out to those horrid pimps. But it still breaks my heart, and they're only scratching the surface." Phoebe struggled to maintain her composure as sadness for the children flooded her heart.

"I know. But we're here now, and we can stay for the rest of our trip if we want to. We don't have to go to the other places we talked about. I'm happy to stay here if you are. And it's not as if they can't use the help," Holly pointed out.

Phoebe nodded. Her friend was right. There were so many other places they could travel to, but the more she thought about it, the more she warmed to the idea of remaining at the mission.

CHAPTER 7

*A*fter patching a few walls around the place, a job Thomas had asked him to do, Nick returned the left-over paint to the cupboard. It wasn't a difficult job, and he'd immediately thought it could have been done by one of the locals, however, he'd done it happily for the man he'd learned to admire greatly since hearing him speak that night at the church.

Thomas was a smart man with a lot of potential. He could be working for a large corporation in Australia, using his skills as an organiser and manager, and yet, he'd chosen to live in Thailand where he was barely making a livable salary as a missionary. He was absolutely devoted to the cause, and Nick admired him for it.

"Thanks, Nick," Thomas said, glancing up from his desk.

"It's nothing, really. Like I said, I'm more than happy to do whatever needs to be done." Scratching his beard, Nick stepped closer to Thomas's desk and folded his arms. "But when you spoke at the church, you talked about the importance of job creation, so I guess I'm feeling a little guilty about doing work you could hire a local to do."

Nick hoped he didn't sound rude, but it had been an issue Thomas had addressed at the meeting. Had he made a mistake in coming if he was simply doing odd jobs anyone could do?

Thomas pushed back in his chair, sighed, and ran his hand through his hair. "I won't lie. It's something I battle with regularly. I mean no offense, but people generally want to come and help rather than provide financial support, so, as much as we'd like to employ locals, we can't afford to. When we go back home and visit the churches, we usually get some decent funding, but there are more pressing needs than painting, and we'd rather use that money for other things, like HIV medications."

Nick frowned. "So, money's what you need more than anything," he said, more to himself than to Thomas.

"That's truly the main thing we need, other than prayer support. It's great that people come and see what we do here, and if they go home and pray because they've seen first-hand the evil and darkness of the sex trafficking trade, well, we're fine with that, as long as they're happy to do odd jobs, like painting, while they're here."

Nick chewed on his lip. He wasn't sure how much good he could do in the prayer department, but he knew his financial situation. Maybe he should have stayed in Australia and simply sent money. But like Thomas had said, seeing it firsthand made all the difference. Despite his misgivings, he felt confident that coming had been the right thing to do, but he knew without a doubt that he'd be financially involved in the ministry upon his return to Sydney.

"Okay," he said. "What else can I do?"

"Any good at fixing washing machines?"

Nick hid a grimace. He knew nothing about washing machines, but he was smart, so he figured it shouldn't be that hard. "I can give it a go."

"Great. I don't know what's wrong with it, but if we can't get it fixed, we'll need to buy a new one, and we can't afford that."

Nick could easily give him the money there and then, but refrained from doing so. "No problem, I'll do my best." He went to leave, but then turned. "Where's the laundry room?"

Thomas chuckled. "I'll show you." Rising from his desk, he stepped around it and clapped his hand on Nick's back. "So, how are you settling in so far?"

"Good, thanks. It's an eye-opener, for sure." Nick shoved his hands into his pockets as he walked.

"It certainly is. When Judy and I first came here eight years ago, our hearts went out to the children and we sensed God calling us to this ministry right from the start."

Nick didn't know anything about how God would call anyone, but he knew that Thomas and Judy had done a great job, and he told him so.

"Thank you, but it's truly not us, it's God who's paved the way. We're simply His hands and feet doing His work."

Once again, Nick struggled to understand that sentiment, but he was impressed by Thomas's humility. Alden and Charity could learn a lot from him.

They turned a corner and went down several stairs before entering the basement. It had a cracked concrete floor and a smell of damp hung in the air, but since the air was so thick with humidity, that didn't surprise him.

"Here's the troublesome machine," Thomas said, stepping towards a large commercial washer sitting in the corner of the room.

"What seems to be the problem with it?" Nick asked, rubbing his hand over it and sounding way more confident than he felt.

"It stops halfway through its cycle. We have to drain it by siphoning the water out."

Nick scratched his head. The problem sounded electrical, and looking at the state of the machine, he wondered if it was worth the effort. He was seriously tempted to give Thomas the money to buy a new one, but in the end decided he'd give it a go. If he had no success, then he might give him the money. "Right. Leave it with me."

Thomas clapped him on the back again. "That's what I like to hear. Let me know how you go."

"I certainly will."

After Thomas left, Nick gulped, and despite the concept of prayer being new to him, sent up a silent request for help. He spent the next few hours pulling the machine apart and trying to work out what was wrong with it. He couldn't see anything obvious, and prayed that when he put it back together, it would work. He was very relieved, and surprised, when it did. Maybe this prayer thing worked after all.

On his way back to give Thomas the good news, he met a young girl and woman in the hallway. The girl, a child of about ten, he guessed, backed away from him. The terror on her face stopped Nick in his tracks. It wasn't just the look of a child afraid of getting into trouble, it was a look of horror, and he'd triggered it.

"I'm...I'm sorry. I didn't mean to alarm you."

The girl quickly hid behind the woman, her face peeking out just enough for him to see her terrified eyes. Feeling terrible, he hated that he'd caused the girl to be so scared. His presence might have triggered unsavoury memories for the child. He was a man, after all. And most of these children had been abused by men.

Unsure what to do, he quickly turned around and found another way to Thomas's office.

"I don't know that I should be here." He slumped in the chair and told Thomas what had happened.

Thomas let out a heavy sigh and clasped his hands together on his desk. "This kind of thing happens often, unfortunately. Don't worry too much, Nick. The girl's nanny will talk with her and assure her you won't harm her. I'm sure the nanny was Maya. She's very good with the newer children."

"But if I triggered that reaction, I must be making it worse for her, and she's already been through so much."

"Not at all. It's important for the children to learn that not all men will hurt them. It's part of their healing process."

Nick raked his hand across his hair. "I still feel horrible. The look on her face..." He'd never seen a little girl look so terrified.

"She'll be okay, Nick. I've got a few minutes before our five o'clock meeting starts. I'll talk with Maya now." Thomas quickly tidied his desk and rose from the chair. "See you at the meeting." As he passed, he clapped Nick on the shoulder. *Again.* Nick wasn't entirely comfortable with the gesture. It seemed too forward when they barely knew each other, but he sensed Thomas had no ulterior motive. It was simply his way of being encouraging.

"Sure." Thomas had told him about the weekly staff meeting being held that afternoon, but he'd been so focused on the washing machine, he'd clean forgotten about it. Thinking it best to stay out of the way to avoid meeting any other children, he wandered into the staff room and poured himself a glass of cold water from the fridge and sat at one of the tables. His first day hadn't quite been what he'd expected, but to be honest, he hadn't known what to expect. It was a far cry from his office on the forty-fifth floor of Barrington Towers, but yet, in many ways, being here seemed more real. Managing a multi-million-dollar company was thrilling and exciting, but it was also ruthless. Here, compassion ruled and people mattered more than anything else. He liked that.

Just before five o'clock, members of the staff began filtering into the room. He'd met some that morning when he arrived, but he'd been told that he'd be formally introduced that afternoon to everybody else. They all nodded and smiled as they entered. There were about twenty in total, several Thai women, a married English couple he'd met that morning, and a number of other westerners. Two young men and three women, including the two he'd noticed sitting together at lunch. For a moment, his gaze connected with the shorter of the two, an attractive brunette who quickly averted her gaze and took a seat beside her taller, blonde friend. His gaze lingered on her a while longer. Not that he was looking for a love interest while he was here, but there was something alluring about her, and he found it hard to take his eyes off her.

Finally, Thomas arrived and everyone grew quiet. He sipped a glass of water and set it on the table before turning his attention to the group. Nick wondered how the talk with Maya and the little girl had gone.

Thomas cleared his throat. "Hi everyone. Before we start, I'd like to welcome our newest volunteer, Nick, who's joined us from Sydney. He's here for a month, and I'd like you to make him feel welcome."

Everyone smiled warmly at him. Shifting in his seat, he nodded and returned their smiles. It was weird. He'd chaired countless meetings over the years, but he'd never felt as welcome in any of those meetings as he did now.

Thomas turned his attention to the two young women Nick had seen at lunch. "Two of our volunteers, Holly and Phoebe, are finishing up their second week. We'd love to hear how you're finding things before we start our discussion. Would you like to share for a few minutes?"

The two women looked at one another awkwardly. After some nervous laughter, the shorter one stood and began speaking.

Her brown hair, tied back in a ponytail, was slightly frizzy. It suited her, and the natural style was attractive. Her skin was tanned, and long, dark lashes framed her blue-grey eyes. She was beautiful, but he sensed her beauty was more than skin deep. He couldn't help but draw comparisons between her and his sister, or Kailey, for that matter.

He listened intently as she spoke, her voice, soft and gentle. "Hello everyone. Well, after two weeks, Holly and I are still here, and we're loving every moment of it, although I don't think it's gotten any easier. Some of the things the children say still break our hearts, but I think the art therapy class the younger children attend is helping them deal with some of their pain."

"Agreed." The other woman rose, standing head and shoulders above her friend. "My students are older than Phoebe's, but it's still heartbreaking to know what they've been through. I think the music classes have been more productive than art for us. Kohsoom plays the guitar and sings with such emotion, it's amazing. Anyway, Phoebe and I are really enjoying our time here, and we're thankful for the opportunity to help in whatever way we can. We feel very blessed."

Nick was touched by their sincerity, and once again couldn't help but draw comparisons between these two women and his sister.

The meeting continued and several important issues were discussed. The mission was seeking to expand their preventative efforts as well as their outreach to the perpetrators. Financial issues were mentioned briefly, but mostly in terms of praying for funding.

Again, Nick listened with interest, wishing he could reassure Thomas there and then that he would help, but he remained silent, not wishing to divulge his identity. However, he did begin making plans. When he returned to his hotel, he'd go online and significantly increase his regular, anonymous donation, but he'd also make a large one-off gift. It was the least he could do.

Thomas continued with a discussion about improving child safety. All volunteers and employees underwent background checks, and foreigners, like Nick, had immigration history checks to see if they'd travelled to Thailand before, which could trigger alarm bells if they had. They couldn't be too careful when it came to keeping the children safe from predators. As he'd undergone this process, Nick had wondered if his identity had been discovered, although he'd stated his occupation simply as manager. He'd be surprised if it hadn't, although no one, not even Thomas, had said anything to indicate they knew who he was.

At the end of the meeting, Nick felt immediately awkward when Thomas suggested they take a few minutes to pray silently before anyone who wanted to could pray aloud. Other than muttering a few quick requests for help, like today with the washing machine, he'd never done this before. The times he'd been to church, the minister had always prayed, so when he closed his eyes, nothing came. His mind was a blank.

He opened his eyes again. Around him, everyone else had bowed their heads and were seemingly absorbed in a conversation with God, but what were they saying? He honestly had no idea, but guessed he should try. Bowing his head again, he closed his eyes. And took a slow breath.

God, I don't know how to do this. I don't even know if You're real, and if You are, who You are. But the others seem to know You, and know what to say, so I'll give it a go. I'm sorry if I say the wrong things. First off, thank You that I'm here. I've already seen how badly damaged these children are, but I've also seen the love that the staff have for them. I pray for that little girl I frightened. I feel so bad about that. I pray for her, God. Help her to know that not all men are dangerous, and if You can, help her to forget the horrible experiences she's been through.

He paused for a moment. What should he pray for next? It seemed that praying was like a shopping list, except he'd left his list at home. It was confusing. What should he be asking God to do? What were the others asking for? And how were they so confident that they could just close their eyes and talk to God and know that He was listening?

He understood how pastors did it. It was their job. They had to sound confident praying in front of their congregations. But for regular men and women like the ones here? Like himself? It seemed weird.

Stumbling his way through a few more phrases, Nick waded through his thoughts until Thomas cleared his throat and began praying aloud. His voice was sincere and gentle, and the way he talked to God was as if they shared a personal relationship. It was the same when a few others prayed. And then Judy finished with words that brought a lump to Nick's throat. "Lord God, bless these little children You've brought into our care. Our hearts break for them, and yet, we know that You're the great healer, and You can turn their lives around and give them a future and a hope, and fill their lives with meaning and purpose. We're Your humble servants, dear Lord. Let us keep our eyes on You and not on ourselves. In Jesus' precious name. Amen."

Nick brushed his eyes quickly, hoping no one had seen the tears gathering, and then he stood while the team began to disperse. When Phoebe and Holly were amongst the first to leave, a twinge of disappointment flowed through him. He'd kind of hoped they might have stopped and spoken with him, especially Phoebe, but he quickly reminded himself that getting romantically involved was not the reason for being here. A few of the other staff chatted with him before they left the room, taking his mind off the women.

Reaching the front door, he bumped into Thomas, who clapped him on the back. *Again.* He liked the guy, but why did he have to do that?

"Hey Nick, I spoke with Maya, and she said the little girl is okay. She's only recently started in rehab, so talking about her reaction to men is part of her healing process."

Nick blew out a breath and shoved his hands into his pockets. "I'm relieved to hear that, although I still feel badly."

"Not the best thing to happen on your first day, I agree. I hope it hasn't discouraged you."

"No. I'll be back tomorrow."

"Good to hear. Enjoy your evening, Nick."

He smiled. "Thanks. You too."

Stepping outside, the humid air enveloped him like a damp blanket. *Tuk-tuks*, cars, motorbikes and bicycles jostled for space on the crowded road. Horns blasted and motorbike engines revved. Although not yet dark, neon lights flashed along both sides of the street as far as the eye could see. It was an exciting place, but also a dangerous one if you were a vulnerable child.

Nick had planned to return to his hotel to eat, but the aroma of freshly cooked Thai food wafting from the restaurants and street carts he passed quickly changed his mind.

He pulled out the pocket guide he'd picked up at the hotel that morning, and selecting a restaurant at random, made his way there.

CHAPTER 8

*A*rriving at the 'Foreign Affairs Café', Phoebe and Holly grabbed a booth in one of the quieter parts of the bustling restaurant. It was their third time there, and they loved the atmosphere emanating from the backpackers, tour groups, and tourists like themselves.

Thomas and Judy had recommended the place early on, saying that as good as it was to dive into the local culture, it was also healthy to be around other expats now and then. It was a way of not burying themselves too much into the mission work and feeling isolated.

The restaurant was large and offered a range of foods to suit every taste, although Phoebe had quickly decided that she preferred the local cuisine to any other. She'd eaten Thai food only twice before the trip, but now she couldn't get enough of it.

"So, what do you think about the concert idea?" Holly asked as she perused the menu. "I'm hoping that at least five of the girls in my class will perform, but it'd be great if some of the other classes got involved, too." Holly had been talking of hosting a musical evening after discovering how talented some of her students were.

"What did Thomas say?" Phoebe was cautious. She wanted to support Holly and her plan, but wondered if it would be beneficial for the girls, or if performing in public would be simply too traumatic.

"He seemed positive. I was a little nervous since we're new, and it's not like I know much about the culture, but he said we could advertise the evening in the local churches and perhaps charge a small entry fee so it would be a fundraiser as well. He seemed to think the local churches would support it."

"Then I think it's a great idea." Phoebe smiled at her friend. "If Thomas approves, then he must believe it would be good for the girls."

Holly nodded. "That's why he suggested only inviting the local churches instead of opening it to the general public. He said they'd be more understanding of the girls' backgrounds and wouldn't judge them for their pasts. Not that it was their fault they got caught up in trafficking, but there's still a lot of stigma they have to fight."

"I'm sure it'll be rewarding for them." Phoebe closed her menu and placed it on the table.

"Exactly. You should see the way they spark up during music therapy. I can only imagine how much it would mean to them to have the community behind them." Holly's own face lit up as she spoke. Like Phoebe, she'd already grown attached to the girls in her class and longed for them to live a life free of the trauma that had haunted them for so long.

A waitress, a beautiful young Thai girl wearing a traditional silk outfit arrived and took their orders. As she was leaving their table, Holly nudged Phoebe. "He's here!"

"Who?" Phoebe frowned, but when she turned to see who Holly was referring to, her breath hitched. It was Nick, the new volunteer. Once again, she was taken by his mischievous eyes. He was drop-dead gorgeous.

Phoebe glanced around the restaurant and chuckled. She and Holly weren't the only women whose gazes were fixed on him. A playful grin spread over Holly's face. "He seems a little lost." Phoebe's eyes widened when Holly stood and invited him to join them.

Her heart beat faster as he approached with Holly. Looking up, she forced herself to smile. "Hi." Her voice squeaked as she pushed the word from her lips. Why was she acting like a giddy teenager? It certainly wasn't how she normally behaved.

"Hi." His easy smile disarmed her further. She had to get a grip.

When he slid in beside Holly, Phoebe knew it would be impossible not to make eye contact with him.

"Phoebe and Holly, right?" he asked, looking from one to the other.

Phoebe gulped and nodded. "Yes. I'm...I'm Phoebe. And she's Holly." She groaned inwardly. Why had Holly asked him to sit with them? There were plenty of others he could have joined.

"I'm Nick. It's nice to meet you. How long have you been in Bangkok?"

Phoebe glanced at Holly, but Holly just shrugged and lifted her brows. Phoebe drew a breath. It was just a conversation, nothing more, nothing less. The fact that it was with a man who had already managed to unsettle her composure was neither here nor there. There was no reason why she couldn't converse with him normally. She smiled. "We've been here two weeks, but we were in Cambodia before then."

"Wow. Cambodia? What was that like?" He leaned forward and she got a whiff of his cologne.

She gulped. "Amazing. I guess it's similar to here, but not as developed. I haven't travelled much, so anything I see is new."

"It's my first time here, too. I can't get over how many people there are."

"And the traffic is mind blowing," Phoebe added.

"I could watch it all day. How they fit so much onto a motorcycle is beyond me." He leaned back against the seat and let out a small chuckle.

Phoebe laughed, relaxing a little. "Me too."

"So, what have you been doing in both places?" He met her gaze across the table, and once again, totally disarmed her. Thankfully, the waitress returned to take Nick's order, promising to deliver his meal at the same time as hers and Holly's. As he thanked her politely, Phoebe pulled herself together.

"While we were in Cambodia, we did some touristy things and visited some of the sights, but we also volunteered there as well. We've spent most of our time so far in Bangkok at the mission."

"Wow. You must have a real passion for helping others if you've given up your holidays to do that."

An image of Reed crossed her mind and the old familiar ache tore through her. Nick had no idea why she'd come, and it was a reasonable assumption he'd made, but she couldn't tell him the truth. Instead, she stumbled through her response. "It's...it's been good seeing new places as well as volunteering. Everything's been amazing. The architecture, the culture, and of course, the food." She wriggled across the seat, needing to get out of there. She flashed an annoyed look at Holly. Why hadn't she helped her out? Holly must have known how uncomfortable she felt. Phoebe drew a breath and apologised to Nick. "You know, I really need to wash my hands. I just remembered that one of the kids was sick and sneezed all over the toys I put away. Please excuse me."

He nodded. "Of course."

She made her way to the bathroom and released her breath. Until now, she'd been doing so well, but talking with Nick had somehow felt like a betrayal to Reed. She knew it was foolish to think of it that way. She'd spoken with plenty of men back home and hadn't thought anything of it, but none of them had affected her like Nick had. Was it wrong to find him attractive? *Was it a betrayal to Reed's memory?*

Phoebe tried to figure her emotions out, knowing she shouldn't live in the past. She'd loved Reed more than anything, but did it mean she would never notice another man? Although Nick was hardly someone to be distracted by. With two months left, she and Holly hadn't fully decided whether or not they'd continue travelling or whether they'd stay at 'Regenerate the Nations'. They hadn't committed to a set period, so they could be gone in a matter of days if they wanted to, and she'd never see him again.

She'd made this trip as a way to heal. Her primary focus was serving others and allowing her own pain to settle. It was no time for getting distracted by a man, regardless of how attractive he might be. With this new resolve, Phoebe washed her hands and made her way back to the table to find Holly and Nick were talking about her concert idea. He seemed supportive.

By the end of the evening, Phoebe felt more comfortable, having decided not to allow herself to be distracted by Nick. She still knew little about him as he'd been the one driving the questions and conversation. In many ways, it was better that way. She didn't need to know anything about him. But it seemed Holly did.

"How long are you planning to be here?" she asked as he reached for and insisted on paying the bill.

"A month. That seemed the most reasonable amount of time I could come for," he replied as he passed his credit card to the waitress.

"I guess you had to take time off work? Were they good about it?" she asked. Phoebe cringed. They didn't need to know his personal business. Why wouldn't Holly stop?

"Yes. My boss is pretty generous about time off." He sounded hesitant, almost as if he was avoiding a direct answer. Maybe he was unemployed? Of course, he wouldn't want to admit that to the two of them when they'd only just met. Especially if the circumstances were something that could have prevented him from working at the mission.

With that thought, Phoebe knew she was looking for excuses to be suspicious of Nick. That wasn't entirely fair. She needed to find a balance. A way to be friendly without being overly interested. Surely she was strong and mature enough to figure something out.

Having settled the bill, the trio stepped outside and went their separate ways, Holly and Phoebe to the guest-house they were staying at, and Nick to his hotel.

As they strolled along the pavement, dodging pedestrians and food carts, Holly asked her what she thought of him. Phoebe tried her best to change the topic, but Holly persisted. "Come on, don't you think he's attractive?" she asked, a playful grin on her face.

Phoebe shrugged. "Of course he is, but I'm not interested."

"I don't see why not. He's one hunk of a man."

"I'm not looking for a hunk, Holly. You know that."

"You *are* allowed to be happy again, Phoebes."

Phoebe blew out a breath. "I know that. I'm not trying to avoid happiness. But perhaps if you're so intent on the man, you should be letting him know you're intrested rather than setting me up." She raised her brow. Two could play at this game.

"Ha! He hasn't looked my way once and you know it. Not only that, but I'm still a fool for someone who'll most likely never return my affections. Just because I can't move on doesn't mean you can't."

Phoebe laughed. "Listen to us. We sound like two school girls."

Holly linked her arm through Phoebe's. "We do, don't we? What's wrong with us?"

"Nothing. We're blessed beyond measure compared to the children we're working with."

"You're absolutely right. That puts everything into perspective."

"It sure does."

As Phoebe lay in her bed that night, she thanked God for the many blessings in her life and asked Him to heal her heart and help her to let go of Reed so she could move on. Not that she wanted to let him go, but she knew she had to. She also pushed any thoughts of Nick from her mind. Well, she tried to, but was finding it very hard not to think of him...

CHAPTER 9

*M*ore than a week had passed and Nick was still committed to the work he was doing at 'Regenerate the Nations'. One day, Thomas had asked him to do some work at the boys' school and suggested he chat with some of the boys who wanted to work on their English while he was there.

It had been a good experience, although rather challenging. The boys had experienced similar traumas to the girls and it was horrific. Nick could hardly contain his anger when he thought about what they'd been through.

When he returned to his hotel in the evenings, he passed a number of massage parlors. He now knew what that was code for. Despite the vibrancy of the city, he felt haunted and entirely distraught by the oppression that lay hidden behind closed doors.

He found himself continually asking God why all of this suffering was happening. If He existed, and was as loving and kind as everyone said He was, why would He allow little children to suffer? Why would He allow young men and women to be so badly abused? *Why was any of it happening?*

He was starting to learn some of the terms often used by Christians, about sin and fallen man and the fact that God had given humanity free will. The existence of evil was not God's fault, but something He allowed so that He could turn the circumstances for His own glory.

But how did that make any sense? How could He be glorified when these terrible things were going on?

Nick did all he could to push the sadness aside. He distracted himself with the work, knowing that at least he was doing something small to help. It wasn't much, but it was something.

And then there was Phoebe. She was proving to be an unwanted distraction, but a distraction he simply couldn't avoid. Along with Holly, they'd shared their evening meal together several times since that first night. He was slowly learning more about her, although she seemed reluctant to share much about herself. He knew she was a kindergarten teacher and a strong believer in Jesus. She also lived in Sydney and had been raised by her mum. He hadn't pressed her about her dad, figuring that whatever had taken her father out of the picture was probably painful.

Whenever Holly, or, on the rare occasion, Phoebe, asked him about his life and family, he gave them vague answers. He told them that he worked in management for a large firm and that he had two siblings, and he'd gone so far as to mention that he'd lost both of his parents a few years back in a car accident.

When asked about his church, Nick confessed that he was still fairly new to church, but that things seemed to have been changing a lot in his life since attending. He told them that he was coming to believe that God was real, but he still had so much to learn about Him.

Phoebe had displayed a twinge of disappointment when he shared that, which puzzled him. Why would that statement have disappointed her? He didn't understand. But Holly had taken the initiative and asked him some deeper questions. Nick began to realise that belief in God had far greater consequences than he'd ever expected. It seemed that it wasn't enough to believe. What to do with that belief was a decision he wasn't yet ready to make.

The day after that conversation, Nick was in one of the empty rooms doing some restorative work on the walls when Holly came in.

"Hey Holly, how are you doing?" he greeted, puzzled as to why she'd be stopping by.

She smiled. "Great, how are you?"

"I'm good, thanks," he replied hesitantly.

"Have you thought any more about the stuff we were discussing last night?" She stepped closer and inspected the wall.

He paused mid scrape. "Quite a lot, actually. I read a bit more of the Bible last night and it's starting to make a little sense, but it's still confusing."

"I can understand that, but if you ask God to open your spiritual eyes as you read, it'll start to make more sense."

"I might try that, thanks." He continued scraping.

"You know, it's really important stuff. We only get one

64

chance at life." Holly folded her arms and leaned against the wall.

"Yeah, I've been thinking about that a bit lately." And he had. Being here had opened his eyes so much, but he'd already been thinking about the true meaning of life before he came. Surely there was more to life than just money, power and material possessions. He had so much, and he was grateful, but something seemed to be lacking.

"It can end so quickly," she stated, shocking him. What was she getting at? He knew life was fragile. He'd lost both his parents. Why would she say something like that to him? Was she trying to force him into making a decision to follow God by scaring him? Surely not.

"I think Phoebe and I truly understood that last year, when Reed died," she continued casually.

"Reed?" He frowned. He'd not heard of anybody called Reed. Had he missed something?

She pretended to inspect the wall. "Phoebe's fiancé."

Nick put the scraper down and turned to face her. "Fiancé?"

"Yes. Phoebe was engaged." She spoke nonchalantly, but Nick sensed she'd planned this conversation specifically to give him the information.

"Wh-when did he pass away?" Nick asked, trying to absorb the news.

"A little over ten months ago. She's still getting over it." Holly turned and met his gaze. "I know she needs to grieve, but I don't want her to be sad forever. She doesn't go after the things she wants because she feels she's betraying Reed."

The penny dropped. Holly was encouraging him to pursue

Phoebe while cautioning him at the same time. She was also explaining why Phoebe sometimes sent mixed signals. "I can imagine it must be hard for her," he said.

"Yes. It's very hard. I think she likes you, but she's hesitant to show it."

He blinked. It was the most unlikely conversation. How should he respond? Of course he'd found Phoebe attractive, but if Phoebe was still grieving the loss of the man she was meant to marry, he could hardly pursue her. And yet, that's exactly what Holly seemed to be encouraging him to do.

Phoebe was also strong in her faith. Would she even consider dating him given that he hadn't made the commitment people kept talking about? He gathered that was a sticking point, but he didn't want to make a commitment just for her sake. If he made it, it would be for the right reason—the last thing he wanted was a fake faith.

But there was no reason why he couldn't be friends with her. He smiled at Holly. "Thanks for all the information. I'll take it on board."

LATER THAT MORNING, while working in the hall outside Phoebe's classroom, he couldn't help but overhear her interacting with the children. She seemed so strong and confident, not at all like a woman grieving. She was obviously stronger than she thought she was, or maybe she got her strength from somewhere else. God, perhaps?

When his parents died, his grief had caused him to do all sorts of foolish things. He hadn't handled it well at all, and he wasn't even that close to them. But Holly had told him that

Reed died only three weeks before the wedding and that they'd been together for two years. They were obviously in love and planning their life together. He couldn't imagine the heartache she must have felt, and was no doubt still feeling.

The way the children responded to her in such a positive way demonstrated what a warm and loving person she was, and that despite her grief, she was able to put others before herself. That in itself made her very appealing, and Nick found himself day-dreaming about her while he patched the wall. So lost in his thoughts, she completely caught him off guard when she appeared in the hall beside him.

A smile flitted across her lips. "I didn't know you were here."

"I've just been patching the wall. I hope I didn't disturb your class." He pulled at his beard that had grown since he arrived and stumbled over his words. All of a sudden, knowing about her fiancé, he felt uneasy in front of her.

"Not at all." Their gazes met and a hint of crimson crept slowly into her face.

Entranced, he couldn't tear his gaze away. Her appeal was not just physical. It was her genuine inner beauty that drew him to her.

One of the children stepped into the hall and grabbed at Phoebe's skirt, ending the moment. She immediately turned to the child and tended to her needs, but Nick sensed that something had clicked between them, that the attraction was mutual. The thought warmed his heart.

At lunch, he was already seated at his usual table when Phoebe entered. His heart rate kicked up a notch when their gazes briefly met before she lined up for her meal, but when she joined him at the table, her gaze remained lowered.

"How was the rest of your morning?" he asked, trying to keep the conversation light.

"Good." She offered a small smile and began poking her food with her fork.

"The kids seem to love you."

Her smile grew broader, but she seemed bashful and didn't look him in the eye. "They certainly respond more than the kids at home."

"I'm...I'm sorry if I made you uncomfortable earlier. It was difficult not to notice how well you interact with the children."

She lifted her gaze slowly to his. "Thank you. And don't worry about it. I was just..." she blew out a breath, "caught off guard, I guess. I didn't know you were in the hallway listening. I appreciate your compliment that I'm good with the kids. And you've been quite a help with all the projects you've been working on."

He laughed. "Thanks. It feels good doing some physical work for a change."

Holly entered and joined them before they could talk more, but Nick was growing more confident that a spark had been lit between them, and he knew that they could, at the very least, be friends, and he liked the thought of that.

CHAPTER 10

lopping onto her bed, Phoebe stared at the ceiling.

"Aren't you at least going to change into your pyjamas?" Holly asked, slipping hers on.

"No use. I don't think I'll sleep much tonight," Phoebe replied.

"Oh no. That's your guilt voice." Holly perched on the edge of the opposite bed. "What is it now? Didn't you teach well enough today, or has it something to do with our lunch companion?" She wiggled her eyebrows and grinned.

"Don't even start," Phoebe moaned.

"I don't have to. You already did." Holly leaned forward and rubbed her arm. "What's up, Phoebes? Want to talk about it?"

Phoebe sat, and crossing her legs, let out a heavy sigh. "I'm not sure what God is telling me. I was so convinced that Reed was the man He wanted me to marry, but then Reed died, and now, here I am attracted to a man who isn't a Christian."

"*Yet.* He told me today that he's been praying a lot and he's realised how much he really does believe in God. I think it's just a matter of time. Maybe you should be praying that he surrenders his life to Christ, and then you won't need to worry."

"Fine, maybe I should, but you know there's more to it than that. I really believed I was meant to be with Reed. How do I move on from that?"

"I don't know that God hand picks our partners, Phoebes. Maybe He does, maybe He doesn't. Maybe it's more about making wise decisions. We know what He expects of us."

Phoebe let out another sigh. "You're most likely right. But it's hard to let go when you've believed something for so long."

"I know. But I think that God's more interested in what happens inside us than what happens to us. Not that He's not interested, but you know what I mean. And you're doing really well."

Tears pricked Phoebe's eyes. "Thank you." She didn't think she was doing well, but Holly's words encouraged her. She missed Reed so much, but maybe she didn't need to beat herself up for noticing an attractive, caring man, especially if that man's heart was open to the Lord. "Maybe I'll get into my pyjamas after all."

"Good. Would you like me to pray for you?"

Phoebe wiped her eyes. "That would be nice. Thank you."

Crossing the floor, Holly sat on the bed and placed her hand lightly on Phoebe's shoulder and began softly. "Dear Lord, bless my friend. Her heart is still heavy with sadness, but thank You for giving her strength to go on. Thank You that through her loss, she's learning more about You and Your ways, and that You're using her to bless others. Fill her with Your peace, and may she know how deeply You love and care for her. And Lord, we also pray for Nick. He's so close to opening his heart to You, so we pray that he, too, might see for himself how broad and deep Your love is for him, and that he will respond by accepting Jesus as his Lord and Saviour. Thank You for bringing him here, Lord. We pray these things in Jesus' precious name. Amen."

"Amen." Phoebe lifted her head and smiled. "Thank you."

Holly pulled her tight and embraced her. "You're more than welcome."

Soon after, once the light was off, Phoebe lay in bed and prayed silently for herself and for Nick. She prayed that God would work in his heart, and that whatever His will was for her own life, that Nick would come to know Him and live his life for Him, because no other decision was more important. Before long, she drifted into a peaceful sleep.

THE FOLLOWING MORNING, as they dressed and prepared for the day, Holly asked Phoebe what her thoughts were about staying at the mission or moving on, given that they still had another two months before they needed to return home.

Phoebe finished cleaning her teeth before replying, taking the few moments to think. As much as she'd like to stay, was it because she felt this was where God wanted them, or for other reasons she didn't want to face? She didn't know. Rinsing her mouth, she dried her toothbrush before putting it back in her toiletry bag and facing Holly. "I'm not sure, Holl. What do you think?"

"I'm tempted to visit that organisation in the Philippines, that Thomas mentioned, but I also don't want to leave here."

"I agree. It's hard to make the choice to stay when there are so many other places that could use our help. But it'd be difficult to leave here, I agree. I've really grown attached to the children."

Holly lifted an amused brow but didn't say anything, but Phoebe knew what she was thinking. It wasn't only the children she'd grown attached to, although she wouldn't admit it. "Let's stay. There's no reason to move on." Holly grinned into the mirror, catching Phoebe's gaze.

Phoebe chuckled. Although there may have been another reason, staying felt right. She would be a friend to Nick and encourage him in his walk with Christ. She would have to battle a growing affection for him, but there was no reason why she couldn't enjoy his company. They were friends, and that was an okay place to be.

ENTERING the mission building a short while later, an eerie silence filled the building instead of the usual happy chatter. Phoebe immediately sensed that something was wrong.

"What's happened?" she asked one of the local nannies when she stepped inside the staff room to make a cup of coffee.

"A rescue took place last night." The woman's eyes moistened as she replied in a soft voice.

"Isn't that a good thing?" Phoebe frowned, puzzled.

"One of the girls not make it. She only sixteen. The owner of the brothel try to fight police and she caught in middle. She die before help arrive. We rescue eighteen, but we grieve for one," the nanny explained.

Phoebe couldn't believe it. That poor girl. It was wonderful so many had been rescued, but how sad for the one who'd died when her rescue was imminent. The injustice was too much. The horror faced by the children and teens they worked with was unimaginable. How unfair that this young woman had come so close to freedom, only to have her life snuffed out at the last moment. Phoebe hoped she'd known Jesus.

The sadness was overwhelming, but the reality was that sex trafficking was happening in Australia as well. It was happening in Britain, in America. Everywhere. She couldn't close her eyes to that fact, but here in Thailand, it was ever present. At least she and Holly had the chance to help in some small way while they were there to make life a little better for those children caught in it, and when she returned home, she'd find a way to help there, too. And maybe, just maybe, God was calling her to full-time mission work, but she still wasn't sure.

The staff gathered together to pray for the family of the young woman, for the rescued girls to heal from their trauma, and also for all those who still needed rescuing.

Sitting on the opposite side of the circle, Nick brushed his eyes as they all raised their heads. Her heart went out to him. It wasn't often that a guy showed emotion like that. When everyone stood to leave, she stepped to him and asked if he was okay.

He shrugged. Shoved his hands in his pockets. "Yes." He let out a large sigh. "Not really. This has gotten to me. As glad as I am about the eighteen, I feel so sad for the girl who didn't make it."

Phoebe nodded. "I know. I'm struggling too. I just hope she knew Jesus."

"Maybe she did."

Phoebe smiled. It was true. No one knew what was in a person's heart other than God. And she was sensing that Nick's heart was opening more to Him each moment.

"Have a good day, hey?" The sincerity in his voice echoed in his smile, and despite the circumstance, made her pulse skitter.

"You too." She returned his smile, and when she walked away, she felt a lightness in her spirit she hadn't felt since Reed died.

CHAPTER 11

*N*ick had been at 'Regenerate the Nations' for almost three weeks. He'd seen Phoebe in so many different situations and was incredibly impressed by her. She was devoted to loving the women and children she worked with and seemed to care about them more than about her own grief.

He wanted the kind of faith that led a person to behave that way. The faith that Phoebe had. Or at the very least, he wanted to understand what it was to be a Christian and to honour God. It still seemed confusing, but he was getting there.

He also wondered if she knew that Holly had told him about Reed. She'd said nothing, but then, neither had he. It was awkward, because how could he raise the issue without intruding, or possibly placing Holly in an uncomfortable situation with her friend?

When he arrived at the mission that day, the little girl who'd been afraid of him on his first day ran up and hugged him. Taken aback, he looked around. The room was filled with nannies, teaching staff, and children. Unsure what to do, he looked down at her and carefully, cautiously, allowed his hand to rest on her back. The little girl said something in her dialect that he didn't understand. He glanced around for someone to interpret.

"She says thank you for making her room so beautiful. It was Pimchan's room you repaired yesterday," one of the nannies translated.

Nick bit back tears. This little girl who'd been so terrified of men was now hugging him. Although what he'd done was so small, it made such a huge difference to her. Enough of a difference to show appreciation to a man who reminded her of her abusers.

Confident that coming here had been the right decision, his heart overflowed at realising he was a blessing to this little girl and had even helped her to heal from a horrid memory. Was it possible that life could work like this? Was this what people spoke about when they said that God could turn even the worst of things around for His glory? Was Pimchan an example of that?

He knelt in front of her and asked the nanny to tell her that it was his greatest joy to repair her room. The young girl beamed at him through a bright smile and beautiful brown eyes.

From that moment on, the day was filled with good things. He'd worked at building a better relationship with the people at the mission, and now they were celebrating with him, it felt good to be acknowledged.

"Hey, isn't that your phone, Nick?" Thomas asked later that

day as a ring sounded from inside Nick's backpack on the floor of the staff room.

"Yeah, it is. Thanks, mate." He'd gotten a local SIM card and sent the number to a few select people from his office in case of an emergency, but this was the first time anybody had contacted him on it.

He rushed over and pulled it out. "Hello?"

"Mr. Barrington, it's Amy."

At the familiar sound of his secretary's voice, Nick's heart plummeted. Stepping out of the room, he lowered his voice. "What is it, Amy?"

"It's the Walterbrook project, sir. I know you said to only call in case of an emergency, but according to the other Mr. Barrington and Miss Barrington, this is a big emergency."

He blew out a heavy breath and raked his hand through his hair. "What's happened?"

She proceeded to tell him about a major funding issue which would require a face to face meeting, the last thing Nick wanted to deal with. But this was major. He had little choice other than to return to Australia as quickly as possible.

Just as he was feeling he'd found his place at the mission, this had to occur. He knew for certain that Alden and Charity wouldn't be able to handle the mess. There was nothing to be done except to fly back over a week early.

He asked Amy to change his flight and let him know the details.

"I will, Mr. Barrington. I'm sorry."

"It's not your fault, Amy."

"I know, but still."

He ended the call and found Thomas. "I'm really sorry, but I have to get back to Sydney. It's a work thing, and a fairly serious matter. Do you think I could come back in a few months and pick up where I left off?"

"Sure. You'll be welcome any time, Nick. It's been a pleasure having you here." Thomas took his hand and gave it a firm shake. "Do you need someone to take you to the airport?"

"Thanks for the offer, but I'll head back to my hotel and pack, then I'll catch a cab. There's no need for anybody to be put out." Nick smiled warmly, trying to assure him he'd be okay. He'd most likely be spending the whole ride to the airport on the phone, and he'd definitely blow his cover if someone from the mission took him, although he was coming to realise that it truly didn't matter if they knew who he was. Still, he felt better that they didn't know, at least for now. Maybe he'd tell Thomas on his next visit.

Nick made his way quickly through the facility, saying goodbye to everyone and promising to return in a few months. He apologised for leaving so abruptly and thanked them for their hospitality.

When he reached Phoebe's classroom, he knocked quietly on the door and poked his head inside.

She looked up and frowned, and after asking one of the nannies to take over reading, she walked to the door. "Are you okay, Nick? You look a little stressed."

He gazed into her concerned eyes, drinking her in. "It's been a hectic few minutes. Can you talk?"

She glanced back into the classroom and then nodded. "For a few moments." She followed him into the corridor.

It felt strange talking to her like this, but he felt he owed her more than a simple goodbye. "I have to go back to Sydney.

Today, if possible. It's all a bit last minute and everything is fine. It's just work stuff."

"Oh my goodness, are you sure everything's alright?"

"Yes, it's just frustrating. My boss will be angry if I don't get back as soon as I can." It wasn't a lie. Alden and Charity were as much his bosses as he was theirs.

"I'm sorry. I had a boss like that once. So frustrating. I hope everything works out okay."

"I'm sure it will. I don't think I'll be sleeping much for the next week or two and this could take months to sort out." He blew out a breath. "I'd like to come back as soon as it's taken care of, but you'll probably be back in Sydney by then."

"Probably." He thought she winced. Was she sad that they might not see each other again?

He steeled himself and asked if he might give her his number. "So you can get in touch with me if you'd like. No pressure or anything. But if you want to, here it is." He pulled a piece of paper from his pocket and scribbled his number on it. He'd never been so anxious about giving a woman his number before, but Phoebe was different. Unlike most women, he guessed his wealth wouldn't impress her. There was no understanding between them and no real reason for her to accept his number, so he was entirely relieved when she did.

"Thank you. I'll call when I get back. It'll be nice to stay friends."

Nick almost blurted out that he'd like to be more than friends, but caught himself in time. Instead, he smiled and said, "I'd like that." He'd always known he'd be leaving the mission before Phoebe and Holly, but he'd expected to have at least another week to get to know her better before he left.

He reached out and squeezed her hand. It was their first physical contact, and it felt nice. No. More than nice. Her hand, soft and warm, fit snugly into his as if they were made for each other. Tempted to draw her close and embrace her, he refrained. Now wasn't the time or the place.

As their gazes met and held, a slow blush rose up her neck and into her face. He gave her hand another soft squeeze and then let go before turning and walking away, his heart beating a crescendo in his chest.

Reaching the street, he hailed a *tuk-tuk* and climbed in the back. All around, traffic rushed by, motorcycle engines revved, cars honked, but all he could think about was Phoebe. Leaving her was agonising. If only they'd had another week they might have parted as more than friends. Would she keep her promise and call? She'd seemed genuine, but she could easily forget all about him. But if she did call, would she be angry at him for keeping his identity hidden, or would she understand? He'd had good reasons, but she might be annoyed and disappointed he hadn't been totally honest with her. It was too late now. He couldn't turn the clock back and do things differently.

His phone rang. It was Amy and she'd gotten him on an eight p.m. flight. There was no time to waste.

CHAPTER 12

*P*hoebe woke the next morning with a heavy heart. Nick was gone, and while she couldn't explain why, she was utterly distraught.

There was no reason to feel so down. She and Nick hardly knew one another, but right from their first meeting, she'd known there was something special about him, and despite her misgivings, she couldn't deny the tingling in the pit of her stomach when he'd squeezed her hand before he left.

While Holly showered, Phoebe opened her Bible and read her daily devotional passage. Focusing on God and His Word was the only way to rein in her wayward thoughts and emotions. After reading the passage, she got on her knees and prayed.

"Dear Heavenly Father, please help me to focus on You today. Help me to grow in Your mercy and grace, and to show Your love to all those around me. Lord, I also pray for Nick. I don't know what to think about him, but I do ask that You reveal Yourself to Him, and that he might come to know You as his personal Lord and Saviour. I sense he's so close, but now that he's returned to his life in Sydney, it would be so easy for him to forget about You, but I pray that You won't let him go. I know how much You love him and desire him to join Your family. Bless him today, Lord God. I pray all these things in Jesus' precious name. Amen."

"Hey, your turn," Holly said, coming out of the bathroom with a towel wrapped around her head.

Quickly pushing to her feet, Phoebe grabbed her clean clothes and stepped into the steam filled bathroom. She turned the shower on, and while the cool water flowed over her body, refreshing her, she pulled her thoughts from Nick and turned them to the day ahead.

THE FOLLOWING FOUR weeks passed in a similar routine. Spending time serving at 'Regenerate the Nations' was both a challenge and a blessing, and Phoebe constantly leaned on God for strength to get through each day. Despite working in the prevention program, she often faced those who'd been trafficked and had become victims. It was heart-wrenching to see such oppression and to hear about some of the awful situations the young girls had experienced.

Thanks to some unexpected, large donations, the mission was able to provide some new opportunities. Thomas and Judy were ecstatic and Phoebe was excited to see their joy.

In their final week, Phoebe and Holly helped with a graduation ceremony for some of the girls who had completed the Regeneration Program. Young women who'd been victims were presented as victors. It was a highly emotional celebration.

Phoebe helped crown the girls as they crossed the stage. Celebrated for their bravery and overcoming their past trauma, they beamed with joy and pride for having finished the first round of intensive therapy.

Following their graduation, some of the girls were returning to their families, while others were going to work in the income generation initiatives offered by the ministry. And the younger ones, of course, would be sent to school and would either return to their families or stay at the ministry, depending on the situation. There were many options, but the goal was always to prevent the girls from having to return to the sex trade while ultimately coming to know Christ.

It was so rewarding for Phoebe to see this work fulfilled. She rejoiced and wept as the young women sang hymns of praise in Thai. "This is by far the most amazing day we've experienced," Phoebe whispered to Holly, her voice choked with emotion.

"Definitely a good note to end on." Nodding, Holly brushed tears from her eyes.

"I don't want to leave," Phoebe said.

"Me either, but we can come back. Maybe not for this length of time, but we can return. We're teachers, after all. We do have breaks."

"You're right. And we will. We have to." Phoebe clapped for the girls who'd put together a worship dance.

The concert Holly had aimed for had come and gone, bringing the community closer and helping the girls gain confidence. Already there were plans for another, and Thomas and Judy decided to make it a monthly worship event. It seemed as though Holly's idea had been a good one.

Three days later, just before boarding the plane, the girls were tempted to change their minds and stay, although they knew they couldn't.

"Thank you for everything." Phoebe smiled as she hugged Judy and Thomas, fighting tears. "We'll be back."

"People say that a lot when they come to visit, but somehow, I believe you." Judy laughed as she returned Phoebe's hug.

Holly slept most of the flight, but Phoebe decided to do some journalling. She wrote out some of her fears about returning home after three months away. Would all the healing she'd undergone in Thailand and Cambodia unravel as soon as she stepped off the plane? The thought of being back in Sydney was strange. Scary.

And there was also the question of whether or not to call Nick. He'd given her his number, but was it wise to call him? To her knowledge, he still wasn't a believer, although more than a month had passed and maybe things had changed. Hadn't she been praying for that, after all?

Was it right for her to bank on that? Was it wrong for her to wonder if God would move in his heart so she could acknowledge her feelings for him? It seemed wrong, and yet Phoebe also knew that her desire for Nick to know Christ was genuine. It was more than just a matter of her having affection for him—she truly wanted him to come to a saving knowledge of Jesus.

The plane finally began its descent into Sydney and Holly stirred from her sleep. Phoebe looked over at her friend who rubbed her eyes and yawned.

"Home?" Holly asked.

"Almost." Phoebe sighed. In many ways, she wished they were still in Thailand.

"Can we go back?" Holly asked pitifully.

"If only…"

Going through immigration and getting their bags checked was easy enough, although it took time. When they emerged, Phoebe was relieved to see her sister waiting for them.

"You're back!" Jennifer squealed, throwing her arms around Phoebe.

"Yeah! We made it." Phoebe returned her hug, but she was tired and less than enthusiastic about being home.

"I want to hear everything, but I'm sure you're both exhausted." Jennifer took Phoebe's carry-on bag and slung it over her shoulder.

"I slept the whole flight, so I'm good, but I'm guessing Phoebe's wiped out. She didn't sleep at all," Holly explained.

"Well, I'll take you both home, and Phoebe, you can rest while I make lunch. How does that sound?" Jennifer asked.

"Sounds good to me," Phoebe replied, yawning.

The drive was mercifully brief, and after dropping Holly at her place, they continued on to Phoebe's apartment. Jennifer helped her inside and then told her to rest a while.

It was so quiet in her room, and she already missed the noise and vibrancy of Bangkok. She never fully made it to sleep before Jennifer knocked on her bedroom door and told her lunch was ready.

Phoebe groaned but got up, and after splashing her face with cold water, joined Jennifer at the table.

"How is it being back home?" her sister asked, passing her

the salad. Two years older than her, Jennifer had been a rock in Phoebe's life after Reed died, despite having a family of her own to care for.

"Climbing into my own bed was great, but I honestly wasn't looking forward to coming home after all we experienced," Phoebe confessed.

"What was it like? Tell me everything," Jennifer urged.

Phoebe inhaled deeply. How could she tell Jennifer everything that had happened in a few moments? It was impossible, plus, she was physically and emotionally exhausted. "I don't think I can right now. It's too much. I mean, there was so much that happened, it's like, how do I even begin?"

"Fair enough. You can tell me everything tomorrow, but why don't you tell me your three favourite things that happened. Three highlights," Jennifer urged before taking a bite of her toasted turkish bread sandwich.

Phoebe thought for a moment and couldn't help smiling to herself. "Well, the first thing was my kindergartners. They were so cute, and their little voices so sweet. They were eager to learn, and when they used their broken English, it brought tears to my eyes."

"That sounds wonderful. So, what else?"

Phoebe let out a slow breath. "I think the second thing is what I learned from Thomas and Judy. They were such amazing mentors and their wisdom was truly awe inspiring. I'm glad I got to spend all that time with them. I learned so much."

"They sounded great from everything you said. I wish I could have met them when they were in Sydney," Jennifer said.

"I'll make sure you do next time they come to town." Phoebe smiled.

"Okay, and the last thing?" Jennifer angled her head expectantly.

Phoebe chewed her sandwich a little longer than necessary, delaying her response. This third favourite thing could lead to a long conversation, one she wasn't prepared for. After swallowing, she took a sip of water and then toyed with her glass. "I...I may have...noticed somebody..." she said cautiously.

"What?" Jennifer's eyes widened. "How come it took this long for you to tell me that part? What is he like? What do you mean by 'noticed'? Is he Thai? Or Cambodian? When did you meet?" Jennifer rushed from one question to the next.

"Calm down! I *noticed* him, that's all. It's not like we're dating. And no, he's not from either of those places. He's actually from Sydney. He heard about 'Regenerate the Nations' when Thomas and Judy were here a few months ago. He was at the mission for three weeks but his boss made him come back early for work."

"He's from here? That's perfect. Too bad he had to come home early. Where does he work?" Jennifer asked.

"I actually don't know," Phoebe confessed. "He seemed fairly private."

"Too bad. What's his name?" Jennifer continued.

Phoebe tugged at a lock of hair before answering. "Nick."

"Nick? Nothing more?"

Phoebe shrugged. "I think I saw his last name once on a planner he carried. It started with a B. Like Barrister, or Barrington," Phoebe said, trying to remember.

"Barrington? Nick Barrington?" Jennifer blinked.

"I'm not sure. It was something like that."

"Phoebe..." Jennifer said, her eyes wide.

"What?" Something about Jennifer's tone made her suddenly anxious.

"Phoebe, was the man you met Nicholas Barrington?" Jennifer asked slowly, holding her gaze.

"Who's that?" Phoebe scrunched her brows. "Why are you acting so strange? Is he a serial killer or something?"

Jennifer pulled out her phone and started searching for something while Phoebe anxiously waited. What had made her sister so serious all of a sudden?

"Phoebe, is this him?" she asked, turning the phone so Phoebe could view a picture.

The photo was of Nick. He didn't have the beard, but otherwise, he looked the same. Except for the suit. And the fact that he was standing on the balcony of a beautiful, luxurious home. "How did you find that photo? Who is he? Why are you acting so serious, and why is he standing in front of a place that looks that amazing?" Phoebe prodded, growing more and more uneasy by the minute.

"He's Nicholas Barrington. A billionaire businessman," Jennifer finally stated.

Phoebe felt her stomach drop. *A billionaire?* A famous man who owned a business? As in, he was the boss himself? As in, he'd come back to Australia because of a crisis in the company he owned? "You've got to be joking," she said through a thin voice.

"I'm not. You managed to land one of the most desired bachelors in the whole country. Now please tell me what you're going to do about it," Jennifer urged, suddenly excited.

Phoebe couldn't handle the confusing thoughts swirling in her brain. How could she not have known? No wonder Nick... Nicholas, had been so private. No wonder he'd been vague when asked personal questions.

Knowing this new piece of information, Phoebe felt certain of one thing. She couldn't call him. She couldn't possibly chase after a billionaire.

CHAPTER 13

"Yes, the reports will be done by tomorrow. I'll double check with my team and get back to you," Nicholas promised before hanging up the phone.

Well and truly back in the workplace, he was still missing Thailand. While he'd drastically increased his giving to 'Regenerate the Nations', he still wished he could be there in person.

Since returning to Australia, he'd not only invested more into the mission, but he'd also looked into other similar organisations, like 'Hesed', the one in Cambodia that Phoebe had mentioned. He found himself researching not just the projects and programs, but the long-term impact, and he also undertook analysis to ensure his money was going to the programs with the best track records.

It was encouraging to read about the impact the best organisations were having in their local communities. And all the ones he'd chosen were Christian ones. That meant something to him now.

He'd become more invested in church as well, attending not just on Sundays, but also the Wednesday evening services, and he was learning more and more each week.

Having seen justice in action, Nicholas was growing in awareness of his own sin and his own need of Jesus. He was learning more about the consequences of sin and that God, being just and righteous, could not tolerate sin, but had paved a way for all mankind to come before Him and be made clean.

The sort of love that was talked about in Scripture was something he'd never comprehended or dared to dream of, until now. It was miraculous and truly something to be in awe of. Was it possible to be loved so completely?

Slowly, he was realising he could.

It was a frightening step to take, accepting the sort of love that promised all of this, but Nicholas knew he wanted it. He wanted it more than he could even express. There was a need deep inside him to be truly loved. To be accepted for who he was as a person, not for his position, his money, his looks, or anything else that swayed peoples' perceptions of him. He just wanted to be loved for himself, like he had been when his parents were alive.

Charity had gone on a few more retreats, and while she returned talking about how great she felt, Nicholas still saw the insomnia and panic attacks barely being kept at bay. He witnessed her surviving on raw food powders and little or no intake of anything solid. He saw her insecurities that presented themselves as pride and arrogance. No matter how she talked about her meditation and peace, he knew it was false.

Likewise, Alden continued to spend money like there was no tomorrow. He rejected responsibility, but enjoyed the title, the cars, the house, and the women. Nicholas saw his emptiness.

When he thought of the faces of little children who'd suffered intense cruelty, children learning about Jesus and being loved, he saw hope. He saw peace and fulfillment. He saw freedom.

How was it that his siblings could be so at odds with themselves, and yet, these children who had nothing and had been so badly treated, were filled with such joy?

The only answer he could think of was Jesus.

When he considered what was stopping him from moving forward and making a commitment, he knew there was one primary reason. He felt like an imposter. He felt so undeserving and worried that if he tried, someone would remind him that he was just a rich boy toying with religion to fill his time. Much like Charity was doing with her meditation and yoga classes.

But the insecurity he felt was something entirely different.

Much of his time was spent thinking about what he'd done at 'Regenerate the Nations' and how fulfilling it had been. While he tried to grasp Jesus with one hand, he clung to the remembrance of Thailand with the other.

His great hope was that his finances were providing things that he wouldn't have been able to help with in person. Perhaps they were being used to hire more local staff and provide additional training opportunities for the children.

At least his donation would help in hiring staff to replace Phoebe and Holly after they left. He tried to remember their timeline and felt certain they should have returned to Sydney by now. Having heard nothing from Phoebe, he couldn't help but wonder if she simply wasn't interested in him.

But that wasn't the impression he'd gotten. Maybe she was just being polite. Or shy. That was absolutely possible.

"Hey." Charity's voice interrupted his thoughts when she knocked on the door to his office.

"Come in." Nicholas waved her in and gestured for her to sit.

"Sorry to interrupt," she apologised, sliding onto the chair and smoothing her skirt.

"No worries. How is everything?" Nicholas asked, clearing his head of previous thoughts and turning his attention to her.

"Good... But I'm realising that this contract could be a bigger issue than I originally thought." Subtle anxiety tinged her voice.

"What makes you think that?" he asked, suddenly feeling uneasy himself. He'd returned to a big mess, but he thought they had it under control.

"I may have found some documents that need to be removed." She fixed her gaze on his.

"Removed?" Nicholas echoed.

"You know what I mean." She gave him a look inferring there were to be no further questions asked.

But he wouldn't be bullied. "No, I don't know what you mean, Charity. What's in the documents? Are you suggesting they need to be destroyed? And if so, what happened to make you decide that's the best recourse?"

"I can have the documents sent to you." She sighed. "I mean, physically brought up. And it wasn't us—it was the contractor. But...I know you. I don't think you'll like what you find."

"Did we do something illegal?"

"No. But the contractor might have. It's difficult language..."

"Charity, you're the head of our law department. It's not difficult language. Not for you, at least. I need you to tell me if we're on the hook for something."

"We very easily could be. I think you should look through the papers and then you can decide what to do about the situation. But if we take it public, the media won't be kind to us," she warned.

Nicholas scrubbed his face with his hands and leaned back in his chair. This was the last thing they needed. "Do you think the media will be any kinder if we're caught hiding something? What did they do, Charity?"

The way his sister held his gaze, he knew it was bad. A muscle in her neck always twitched when she was anxious. Right now, it was pulsating. She pursed her lips and then answered, "They charged the client for five reports that were totally fabricated."

Icy fingers seeped through every pore of his body as he digested the information. How had they engaged such a dishonest contractor? They weren't talking small amounts. Each report would have cost the client hundreds of thousands. "How did this slip through, Charity?"

She shrugged off-handedly while pulling absent-mindedly at a thread on her skirt.

Nicholas seethed. While he'd grown a lot in his personal life in the previous months, his professional career was in a dire situation. Trying to deal with this whole mess regarding their contractor had been difficult enough without these new legal issues coming to light. "Bring me the documents. I'll figure it out." He determined not to let his frustration and disappointment get the better of him.

"Okay. Just remember we're better off keeping this quiet and dealing with it as an internal matter," Charity said as she rose from her chair.

As Nicholas watched her go, he felt very little satisfaction in what she'd said. If this was a legal matter, it couldn't be shoved under the carpet, because issues had a habit of coming back to bite. He wouldn't allow the company his grandfather had begun and had been so proud of to come into disrepute. Not on his watch.

For a moment, he thought how nice it would be to not have this responsibility. To instead be like Thomas and Judy in Thailand, doing something more personally rewarding. Not that they didn't have their challenges, but it was different.

However, that wasn't his life. His life was here, working at the firm with his siblings, watching and wondering when the next tower might come crashing down on them all.

Before long, Charity was back in his office with the documents in hand. She still seemed churlish, like she knew he'd do the right thing and she desperately didn't want him to. She'd be aware, just like he was, that disclosing the fraudulent reports could destroy not only the contractor's business, but their company as well.

"Are those them?" he asked, reaching out a hand to take the papers from her.

"Yes. And I'm wishing I didn't report any of this to you. I know you. You'll disclose it all and come clean. It's not just about you, though. It's about all of us. Remember that," she said, giving one final warning.

"Sit," Nicholas ordered, ignoring the fact that she clearly wanted to vacate the room.

"Please…" she said quietly.

"Sit down, Charity," he said in a tone that let her know she'd better not argue.

Nicholas skimmed through the first couple of pages. It was true. Their contractor had fabricated the information in the extra reports. It was all there in black and white if you knew what you were looking at. What was more, these documents proved that someone in the company was aware of it already.

Doing something about the issue would mean, for a certainty, that the business would come under heavy scrutiny. They could attempt to hide it. No one would ever have to know. But it didn't align with Nicholas's growing conscience. It didn't align with his developing understanding of God's justice. Yes, it would be better for their business, but it wouldn't be better for his soul.

He met his sister's gaze. Disappointment registered on her face. How long had she been aware of this? Was that why she was so nervous? Had she been a part of it? "So, you think we ought to settle the matter internally?" he asked.

"It makes sense to me. We can get the proper reports prepared and keep them on file, and when any audits take place, everything will be in order."

Leaning forward, Nicholas crossed his arms on the desk and held her gaze. "You know as well as I that it doesn't work that way, Charity. And if we try that, it's only going to get us called out. Someone will notice that the reports are different.

It's not a good idea, and I won't have it in this company. I hold the majority shares, so I get the final say. We'll handle it the right way. We'll get the new reports prepared, and they'll also be given to the client. He'll know the initial reports he was given were fabricated."

Her jaw tightened. "As long as you know that we might all go down, do whatever you think," she added bitterly.

"I'm left with no choice," he said quietly.

"You could choose to protect your family." Her voice was laced with sarcasm.

"It would only cause harm in the long run. Trust me, Charity. This is what we have to do. I don't like it any more than you do, but we have no choice. This is how it goes," he told her again.

"Then so be it," she snapped. "What do you want done with the documents?"

"Put them on a flash, then bring me the flash and the originals. I have a couple of people to talk to."

Tight lipped, she nodded and left the room.

Nicholas slumped in his chair and blew out a heavy breath. How had all of this happened? Leaving Thailand had been difficult enough, but coming back to this mess was a nightmare.

An image of a classroom in Thailand and an attractive volunteer English teacher flitted through his mind. If only he could go back and leave all this behind.

CHAPTER 14

*A*fter discussing the contractor issues with several trusted advisers, Nicholas decided to put into action a plan he'd started making days before. It was time to find Phoebe and tell her exactly what was on his mind. Plus, he needed a breather from the nightmare unfolding on the forty-fifth floor of Barrington Towers.

Visiting Phoebe at her school was a huge risk, but Nicholas decided it was worth it. Pulling up in his car, he hoped he wouldn't be too conspicuous. He'd always preferred more subtle vehicles than his siblings, but his Porsche still stood out in certain parts of town. Mercifully, in this part, his car was the norm. Porches, Mercs and BMWs lined either side of the street.

He'd done some sleuthing and found the school she taught at, and had driven there in the hope she might be happy to see him. It concerned him that she hadn't called, but she'd made such a huge impression on him in such a short amount of time while they were together in Thailand that he couldn't leave it go. He had to see her again.

The bell marking the end of the school day rang and children began pouring out, but he had no idea what time Phoebe would leave. Would she stay twenty minutes? Two hours? Surely he'd need only wait a short time before she exited.

But when half an hour had passed, he was starting to feel like he ought to have called her first. Maybe it would have been wise to gauge her interest before stalking her. *Was he crazy?*

A knock sounded on his window, startling him.

"Excuse me, sir. Are you waiting for someone?" The older female appeared quite concerned. He guessed she had a valid reason.

"Uh, yes. I'm here to meet with Phoebe Halliday. She's a friend of mine," he said, trying to sound more confident than he felt.

The woman's brows knitted together.

"I promise I'm not here for any other intention. Just to see Miss Halliday," he reiterated.

The woman pursed her lips. "Right. Let me see if I can find her."

"Thank you, I appreciate that."

"Is she expecting you?"

"No. It's a surprise. But don't worry. Like I said, she's a friend, but we haven't seen each other in over a month. I'm simply looking forward to surprising her."

"I don't know that Miss Halliday is the sort to readily accept surprises from gentlemen," the woman muttered under her breath.

"Yes, well, we'll have to see, I suppose. I think she'll be fine when she sees me. Surprised, for sure, but I think she'll be pleased."

When the woman walked away, presumably to get Phoebe, Nicholas decided a few words of prayer wouldn't go astray. He still wasn't sure about this prayer thing, but he'd been doing it more often of late. It felt strange talking to someone he couldn't see, and he didn't know if God heard him or not, but it was worth a shot. Especially when so much was at stake.

Bowing his head, he asked God to grant him favour and give him this opportunity to get to know Phoebe a little better. He also asked God to strengthen him and to help him with all of his struggles to believe.

He didn't want to make a commitment to become a Christian just for Phoebe's sake, but he did want to know God better and he also wanted to know Phoebe better. While the two were unrelated, he couldn't deny the fact that the former would certainly be a benefit to the latter in the long run.

He felt strengthened after praying. Although he had no real idea if God heard him or not, every time he tried to pray, he often felt a peace and strength he'd not experienced before, so maybe his prayers were being heard.

It was no different this time. He felt energised, although there was no telling how long it would last, and if it would dissipate the moment he saw Phoebe. But right now, strength surged through him and he had a sense he wasn't alone.

After a few moments, he saw her coming out of the building. She was wearing a soft cream blouse and dark trousers, and her hair bounced on her shoulders.

His heart pounded. She looked more beautiful than he'd ever seen her, but she wore a frown on her face. Feeling hot and sweaty when the older woman accompanying Phoebe pointed to his car, he undid the top button of his shirt and loosened his tie.

Phoebe hesitated. He didn't blame her. She had no idea who was waiting for her, so he had no choice but to get out. Not wanting to frighten her, he opened the door and hesitantly climbed out and stood beside the vehicle, watching her expression as recognition dawned on her face.

It quickly became evident that she knew it was him, but she didn't seem as thrilled as he would have liked. She seemed uncomfortable and maybe even a little annoyed.

He waited for her to start forward before he made a move. His palms grew clammy and his heart beat double time.

She walked slowly towards him. He wanted to know everything that was going through her mind in that moment, but he was also terrified. Maybe she wasn't a fan of grand romantic gestures. Maybe she was the sort of woman who liked to be slowly wooed. He should have called first.

But she continued towards him, so he closed the car door and met her halfway. Reaching her, he smiled nervously. "Hello, Phoebe."

Obviously puzzled, she gave him a polite, if somewhat cool, nod.

It was like a slap to the face. She didn't want to see him. *How had he gotten it so wrong?*

CHAPTER 15

"What are you doing here, Nick?" Phoebe asked as she approached the man she never expected to see again. She wasn't angry. Well, maybe a little. Nick had been less than honest with her back in Thailand, but she wasn't mad he'd shown up. Merely shocked.

"Yes. I'm sorry. I should have called first." He rubbed the back of his neck, and despite herself, she felt a little sorry for him.

"I'm just surprised to see you here, that's all."

"You didn't call." As his eyes lifted and met her gaze, there was an involuntary tingling in the pit of her stomach, and for a moment, instead of seeing a smartly dressed man standing in front of a Porsche, she saw a bearded man in Thailand standing in front of a mission building.

But Nick was a billionaire, and that changed everything. She gulped. "No, I didn't. You didn't tell me who you were."

His mouth opened. "You know who I am?"

"Yes," she replied curtly.

"Is that why you didn't call? Because of who I am?"

Phoebe paused. His question was a challenge. He wasn't asking if she'd ignored him because he hadn't told her who he was. He wanted to know if she'd ignored him because of who he was. Was she so shallow that she'd reject him based on his financial situation?

She winced. "I don't know. I wish I could say it was because I was annoyed you hadn't been totally honest with me. But in truth? I had no idea how to act around a billionaire. I didn't know how to talk to you once I knew who you were. How could I?" She felt like a fraud. Was she not a Christian? How could she have judged him on the basis of his financial position?

"Then you understand why I didn't share more about it," he replied quietly.

Phoebe felt her cheeks warm in shame. He was right.

"I don't like being judged on my having money. It frustrates me that people can never see beyond that. I'm more than the wealth my family inherited. I'm more than my grandfather's business. But people don't see that. So yes, I kept my true identity quiet because I didn't want you to be yet another young woman seeing the same."

Phoebe's blood started to boil. She could take his words the wrong way and twist them into an insult. *You think I'm shallow like those other girls?* But she pushed the thought away. It wasn't what he meant. And even if it had been, it wasn't entirely unfounded. She really had judged and made up her mind about him when she learned the extent of his wealth.

"I'm sorry for passing judgment on you based on your finances," she whispered, somewhat reluctantly.

A lopsided grin spread across his face. "Apology accepted."

For a moment, Phoebe felt annoyed. How had this been turned around on her? How had it gone from Nick being secretive about his identity, to her apologising for judging him? But God was convicting her. Yes, Nick had made a mistake in hiding his identity, but just because he was wealthy didn't mean that God didn't love him as much as He loved those who had nothing. Surely it was just as wrong for her to pass judgment on him as it had been for him to mislead her about his identity.

And now she could understand why he'd done it. It wasn't hard to see how difficult it must be for him. Of course he would want to keep his wealth quiet.

He looked at her with his clear blue eyes. "Now we've got that sorted, would you like to have dinner with me?"

The question threw her. As far as she knew, he still wasn't a Christian. It was very important to her that any potential life partner hold the same spiritual values as her. And how could she agree to a date with this man she knew so little about? Although, if she were honest, Nick still dominated her thoughts. *But was he a good man? Could she trust him?* She drew a deep breath and released it slowly while studying him. "You're inviting me to dinner?" she repeated.

"Yes." His gaze was as soft as his voice, totally disarming her.

"Right…" The word drifted from her mouth.

"Is that a 'yes' right? Or a 'I can't believe you're asking me for dinner' right?" He appeared to be holding his breath.

She couldn't believe this was happening. Nicholas Barrington, billionaire businessman, was asking her to dinner. She let out a tiny giggle. "Of course it's a 'yes' right!

"Really?" His eyes lit up, almost in disbelief.

"So long as you promise there'll be no more secrets, then yes, I'm happy to have dinner with you."

"There is something more." He visibly gulped.

"More? Like what?"

"I was wondering if, not only could we do dinner, but could I visit your church? I like the one I'm at, but I'm curious about yours."

She was entirely taken aback. Nick wanted to go to her church? He was taking an interest in something really important to her, even though he already attended elsewhere? "You want to come to my church with me?"

"Yes. It's nothing against the one I've been attending, but I think there are other churches that might challenge my perspective further."

Phoebe chewed on her lip. Talking like that, about perspective, indicated to her that he truly didn't understand what the gospel message was all about, and she wondered what his church was like. Was it the sort that really preached the truth, or was it one that watered the gospel message down, but in doing so, left people wanting more? Whichever it was, it was enough to make him hungry.

But she had other concerns. Not ones she was willing to share with him, like what if the church folk didn't respond well to him? Reed's friends, his parents. How would they all respond if she brought a famous billionaire with her to church so soon after Reed's passing? Would they be supportive, or would they think she was betraying his memory?

It had been just over a year, and while most days she still couldn't believe the reality that Reed was gone, she also knew she had to move forward. She couldn't hold onto her grief forever.

She cautiously nodded. "Yes. You can come to church with me. It's the one on Crossview. It's fairly small and old, but it's visible from the road."

"I know it. That's where you go?"

"Yes. The service starts at nine o'clock. We can meet there."

"Perfect. And maybe we can go to lunch afterwards."

Phoebe nodded, still struggling to believe this was happening. "Sounds like a good idea. I think it's a better option for now than going to dinner."

Nick smiled broadly, clearly relieved by her responses. "All right. Until Sunday, then."

She returned his smile. "Until Sunday." But as he drove away and she walked to her car, her internal debate returned. Nicholas Barrington was the most eligible bachelor in town, according to Jennifer, and she was taking him to her church. What was she thinking? *God, is this madness, or what?*

CHAPTER 16

*N*icholas woke early on Sunday morning, anxious about what the day ahead would hold. Deciding to go for a jog in the hope it might settle him, he quickly threw on his running gear and headed out.

At this time of morning, the streets around his area were almost deserted, just a few cyclists, another jogger, a young woman taking her dog for a walk. A far cry from the hordes of people and traffic he would have passed if he'd been in Bangkok instead of Sydney.

After running for almost a full hour, he returned home and jumped into the shower before dressing carefully, selecting the plainest clothes he owned, beige trousers and a white button-down shirt. More than anything, he wanted to blend, not stand out.

He arrived at Phoebe's church ten minutes early, just like she'd asked him to. As soon as he parked, she pulled in behind him in her car.

Before opening the door, he took several deep breaths. Once or twice since surprising her the other day at her school, he'd almost called to cancel. As much as he wanted to be with her, he didn't really know her, yet here he was, about to walk with her into her church. And it was so small, he wouldn't be able to hide. He'd made a mistake. But how could he leave now? His heart thumped wildly. She was out of her car and walking towards his.

Steeling himself, he opened the door and smiled. She looked gorgeous in a knee-length floral skirt, and her hair glistened in the sunlight, giving it a rich glow. "Great timing," he said with a nervous laugh.

"Yes." She returned his smile. A good start. "Thanks for coming early. As you can see, a lot of people are arriving already, and I wanted to go over a few things with you." She glanced over as another car drove in, but after lifting her hand in a quick wave, she turned back to him. "Since it's not a large church, it's going to be difficult for you to be anonymous. I'll introduce you by your first name, but I wouldn't be surprised if a lot of people recognise you. Even though I didn't."

He nodded slowly. He didn't like hearing that, but he understood. It was difficult to go anywhere incognito since he and his company were often in the news. Especially recently. "I understand," he replied, running his hands down his trousers.

"Are you worried?"

"Not worried so much as anxious."

"I'm sure it'll be fine. Come on." Phoebe nodded her head towards the door.

He walked beside her and kept his gaze low. He noticed a

few stares and a couple of whispers. Phoebe also seemed to be trying to shrink. They slipped into a row near the back.

There couldn't be more than a hundred people in the chapel. The church he'd been attending had well over a thousand. It was easier to hide there than here. But this church meant a lot to Phoebe and he knew there must be a good reason.

The music started, and while some of the songs included language from centuries past, he grasped such depth and intensity in the lyrics that he'd never experienced at his own church. It was like God teaching him something new and unreal through the words.

When the hymn ended, the pastor stood. After thanking God for His Word, he began to preach, and Nicholas felt the veil lift from his eyes.

Whatever he'd been trying to grasp, this was it. Suddenly, within reach, was a Jesus he couldn't have fathomed. A Jesus who'd given up all He had in heaven with His Father, to come to earth as a human to rescue mankind from sin. The pastor quoted John chapter one, verse fourteen, *'And the Word became flesh and dwelt among us, and we have seen His glory, glory as of the only Son from the Father, full of grace and truth.'*

Grace and truth! That was it! The fact that God demanded justice but had already issued it in the personhood of Jesus. That Jesus, completely God and completely man, had voluntarily come to earth to be the solution to mankind's separation from God for all those who believed.

He'd not heard the gospel presented like this before, but it was so obvious now. How had he not seen it when he'd read through the Gospel of Matthew on his own?

Then the pastor talked about how Jesus' coming had been foretold in the Old Testament, and, all over again, Nicholas felt completely overwhelmed with joy. If everyone heard the truth put this way, he felt certain that no one would ever reject it! How could they? It was an amazing act of love. A plan that God had had from the very beginning, even when He knew that His precious creation would reject Him and sin would take over their lives and cause them to do despicable acts, like trafficking young children. This was His plan of salvation! A way for sinful mankind to have a relationship with a holy and perfect God who loved His creation with an unrelenting love, and who just wanted them to love Him back.

Towards the end of the service, Nicholas found himself on the brink of tears. He didn't want to weep in front of everyone, especially not Phoebe, but the goodness of God as it had been presented that day finally made sense. God was reaching out to him, and had been since the beginning of time. The gospel message was so much greater than he'd ever expected.

As the pastor closed the sermon, praying a prayer over the congregation, Nicholas brushed his eyes and mentally prepared questions to ask Phoebe after the service.

After the benediction, when everyone stood and began chatting with each other, Phoebe introduced him to a few of her friends. He almost wished they could slip out like he normally did, but that wasn't going to happen.

"And these are Mr. and Mrs. Fisher," she said, her voice suddenly edgy.

Mrs. Fisher, a kindly, middle-aged woman, took his hand and shook it warmly. "It's so nice to meet you, Nicholas." Her husband greeted him equally warmly before turning to Phoebe and giving her a fatherly kiss on the forehead which Nicholas found strange.

After the couple had gone, Nicholas asked her quietly about them.

She let out a small breath. "They're the parents of my—of Reed," she said, softly.

"Oh. I'm sorry. If I'd known, I would have made more of an effort." Although they hadn't spoken about Reed, from the way she looked at him, he knew that Holly had told her about their conversation.

"I'm glad you didn't. They were supportive enough as it was. I'm glad you were just yourself."

"And that's all I want to be."

"What did you think of the service?" she asked as they made their way to their cars.

"It was amazing. I have so many questions. Shall we take my car to lunch? That way we can chat while we drive."

"Sure." When she smiled, her face lit up and his pulse quickened. She radiated a vitality that drew him like a magnet.

They drove to a nearby restaurant. It wasn't overly fancy—he wanted her to feel comfortable for their first date. Walking up the stone stairs bordered on either side with palm branches swaying gently in the warm breeze, he felt exhilarated, filled with anticipation. The building was of Mediterranean style, and they chose a table in the alfresco area overlooking the city.

The waiter poured water and took their orders. Seated opposite Phoebe was a dream come true. But he still had questions. "What about that other passage the pastor quoted? From Isaiah, I think it was."

"Yes. That's a great passage. Jesus was prophesied to come

throughout the whole of the Bible. We split it into Old Testament and New Testament because of the Covenants, but the whole thing points to Jesus. It's amazing."

Nicholas grew more and more fascinated. He felt energised in his spirit as he was learning something far greater and of more importance than anything else.

As they shared the pizza oozing with mozzarella, sun-dried tomatoes and olives, they chatted easily about topics he'd never expected to talk with anybody about so freely. Phoebe's faith was genuine and deep, and she had great understanding of her beliefs. It was easy to forget they were on a date, but when the waiter delivered their coffees and their gazes met and held, he knew he was falling for her. He wanted to reach out and touch her hand, but it was too soon.

"Tell me about your childhood, Phoebe. Where did you grow up?" he asked after the waiter left.

"Around here. My life is boring compared to yours."

"I don't think anything about you could be boring. You're the most interesting woman I've ever met."

She let out a bashful chuckle. "I'm sure you don't mean that."

"I do. You're an amazing woman." He held her gaze, totally entranced by her compelling personage.

Her face pinkened slightly before she averted her gaze. He didn't want to embarrass her. He needed to be patient. Not push. And besides, there was something he needed to do.

He gulped. "Phoebe, I want to become a Christian. I want to experience God's grace and love for myself, and I want it to be a part of me."

Her gaze shot up, her eyes wide. "That's wonderful, Nick!"

He took a deep breath. "Will you tell me what I need to do?"

"Absolutely. Just say what's on your heart. God will hear you. Would you like to take a walk?"

He nodded. Taking a walk was a great idea. They stood, he paid for the meal, and they stepped outside. A park was nearby, so they headed for that, stopping to sit on a park bench alongside a small pond.

His heart was expectant as he bowed his head and drew a steadying breath. Phoebe placed a hand on his shoulder as he prayed. "Lord God, I'm a sinner in need of Your saving grace. I praise You that even though You're the Creator of the universe, You loved me so much that You sent Your perfect Son to earth that I might have new life. Thank You for Your mercy and grace. Renew my heart, oh Lord. Make it soft and pliable, and help me to live my life in a way that will bring glory and honour to You. I want to love and serve You forever."

"And Lord," Phoebe said softly, her hand light on his shoulder, "I ask that You bless Nick. Bless him for making a stand for You. Let him see how much You truly love him, and fill him with Your peace. Thank You for his kind heart, and may You use him in whatever way You see fit to extend Your Kingdom. I ask this in Jesus' precious name. Amen."

Opening his eyes, he smiled. His heart was light and his spirit free. This was the beginning of his new life.

CHAPTER 17

hree weeks had passed since Nick had made his commitment to Christ, and Phoebe was glad they'd begun dating after that. She was amazed at how eager he was to know Jesus more.

The integrity he showed in every aspect of his life and business wowed her. When a story broke in the media that he'd come forward with information about illegal activity in his business, it was clear that the company could be in trouble. But by addressing the issue early on, it seemed the company had avoided some of the backlash, although there was likely more to come.

She couldn't help but respect Nick for being so willing to put everything on the line to make things right. She'd seen him grow under the discipleship of her church in just a few weeks, and he'd already joined a men's Bible study and was getting to know her pastor.

And yet, there were some things in the relationship she still couldn't get used to.

"Oh...wow," she said in shock upon opening a gift at dinner one night. He'd bought her another perfume. Another designer perfume. As a woman who'd always opted for whatever was cheapest but still smelled nice, she wasn't used to these thick glass bottles with Italian names sprawled across them. She wasn't accustomed to anything that cost more than a few dollars.

But Nick was treating her like a queen. And he wooed her with special things on almost every date.

The restaurants they went to had also started moving up in class. It was nearing the point that she wasn't sure what to wear anymore, because she always felt underdressed whenever they went out. Sometimes she made comments about not being dressed well enough, but Nick always brushed them off and told her she looked beautiful and that she was dressed perfectly. It was sweet of him, but she didn't think it was entirely true.

It was sweet the way he was going so overboard, but it wasn't anything she was used to and she didn't know if she particularly liked it.

When she opened the perfume, she knew she had to say something. Concern about hurting his feelings or appearing ungrateful had always held her back. But it was too much for only three weeks together.

"Nick, this is lovely," she began. He smiled, obviously pleased that she liked it. "But you don't have to give me gifts on every date."

His expression faltered, but it was clear that he was willing to listen and he really cared about what she thought.

"I love the earrings and the perfumes and the chocolates, but if you just want to get me flowers once every few months, I'd be more than happy," she commented carefully.

"But flowers die."

"They do, but they're beautiful while they're alive. You don't have to do all of this, seriously. I'm thankful, please don't get me wrong. I'll wear the perfume, but I want you to know that I'm dating you for you, not for your gifts, or any other reason."

Nick blew out a small breath. He enjoyed giving her gifts— he didn't give them out of obligation. Maybe she shouldn't have said anything. But no, she'd needed to. "I really appreciate all of it, Nick. I'm grateful, I truly am, but I'm happy just being with you."

He reached across the table and squeezed her hand. "I'm sorry, Phoebe. Hearing that makes me happier than you know, and I didn't realise I was overdoing it. In my experience of dating, most women have only wanted me for my money and gifts, so dialing it down is a new thing for me."

She chuckled. "Like I said, flowers every now and then is more than enough." Dating Nick, she'd been filled with unique emotions. She was still coming to terms with the fact that she was dating someone after having lost Reed. But everyone had been surprisingly supportive. Reed's parents and friends, her church family, they'd all encouraged her.

Jennifer, and even her own mother, had been thrilled to know she was dating someone and allowing her heart to heal. Phoebe convinced Jennifer not to tell their mother who Nick was until they'd been dating a few more weeks, but when she found out, she was shocked, but also in awe.

Holly continued to be excited every time Phoebe reported a date back to her. She was still completely stunned and embarrassed that she hadn't figured out who he was when they were in Thailand together.

But dating Nick had come with other challenges. He closed up when his family became the topic of discussion. His unwillingness to share anything much about his family life bothered her. He rarely spoke about his parents, only that they'd been killed in a car accident fifteen years earlier. There was a lot of healing to be done in his heart, but she was confident that in time he would feel comfortable enough to share with her.

Despite working with his siblings, she gathered they didn't get on. She asked to meet them, but he told her she wouldn't like them, so she let it go. But it wasn't easy and often left her confused. She would have liked to meet them. They were his family, after all.

And yet, every time Nick showed up to take her on a date, all of these things were forgotten. She swooned when he smiled, but then later felt a twinge of guilt for letting go of Reed so easily.

Was it alright? Was she supposed to move on like this? Everyone had encouraged her to do so. She was falling in love with Nick, but was it really okay?

When he picked her up for their next evening out, he brought her a bouquet of pink carnations and she was so thankful he'd listened to her. She inhaled the sweet smell and then kissed him on the cheek.

After Reed, it had been difficult to consider a real kiss. She was moving slowly in the relationship, but Nick had patiently followed her lead, although she knew he longed for more, as did she. But she wasn't ready. And for a woman not yet ready, Nicholas Barrington was the perfect gentleman.

CHAPTER 18

*N*icholas tried to dress as casually as he deemed appropriate. Phoebe had warned him not to overdo it for the visit to her mother's place, but nevertheless, he wanted to appear respectful and gentlemanly.

Looking in the mirror at the blue short-sleeved button-up shirt and tan slacks he'd chosen, he still felt a little overdone. Or maybe the outfit wasn't nice enough? He sighed. Was it possible that it was too dressy and not dressy enough at the same time?

He was glad Alden wasn't here to see this. His brother would mock him, for sure, since this sort of anxiety over his appearance was unlike him. But meeting Phoebe's mum was an important step. They'd been dating for nearly three months and he already knew that he cared about her enough to make a commitment.

But if Mrs. Halliday didn't like him, the relationship would be over. Phoebe would let him go. Her mother was so important to her, and when all was said and done, he was just a man she'd recently met. The choice, if it came to that, would be a no-brainer for her.

Finally settling on his outfit, he slid into his car and drove to Phoebe's place. When he arrived, he asked her if he was dressed appropriately.

"You look perfect." She smiled while her gaze swept over him from head to foot.

"Really?"

"Yes." She chuckled. "You know, Mum's nervous about meeting you, too. She's never met a billionaire before."

He let out a small groan. "You told her I'm just an ordinary person, didn't you?" He stepped forward and took her hands while gazing into her eyes.

A coy smile grew on her face. "Quite the opposite, actually. I told her how special you are...to me." She gave him a quick peck on the cheek before ducking under his arm and sprinting to his car. He ran after her. When he reached her, he was tempted to wrap his arms around her and kiss her, but he knew she wasn't ready. Instead, he opened the door and waited for her to slide in.

Sitting beside her, his hands grew clammy.

"Just be yourself, Nick. Relax. The more you relax, the more comfortable Mum will feel."

How could he possibly relax when he was meeting someone as important as her mother? The future of their relationship depended on whether she warmed to him or not.

"What was that Bible verse the pastor quoted on Sunday? Something about the peace of Christ?" he asked.

"Colossians three, verse fifteen? *'And let the peace of Christ rule in your heart, to which indeed you were called in one body. And be thankful.'"*

"You have it memorised?"

"As of this morning. I've been working on it all week. I needed peace as well."

"About this dinner?" He turned and faced her.

She released a slow breath. "No, just everything. Life is in such a different place than I ever imagined it would be."

She was right. She was supposed to be married to another man, not taking him to meet her mum. He wondered if sometimes she wished it had turned out according to her original plans.

"I think, in some ways," she continued, staring out the window, "I'm worried God is going to take all of this away from me, too."

Frowning, Nicholas let go of the steering wheel with one hand long enough to give her hand a gentle squeeze before returning it to the wheel.

"I didn't imagine I could find happiness again."

He felt her gazing at him. He glanced at her once and smiled, but considering how Reed had died, he was reluctant to take his eyes off the road for long.

"I guess I'm surprised I could ever feel happier than I did before." She breathed the words out, sounding relieved. As if it was the first time she didn't feel guilty for feeling happy.

"You're happier?"

"I am. But I'm starting to understand that happiness is a feeling that can change day by day depending on circumstances, but true joy comes from having peace, regardless of the circumstances, and only God can give that."

"Wow. That's deep. I'm going to have to mull that over," Nicholas said.

They finally reached Phoebe's mother's home in the suburbs. Nicholas pulled his Porsche into the driveway of the tidy, but small bungalow. He switched off the engine and climbed out before opening Phoebe's door for her. While she stepped out, he grabbed a box of chocolates from the back seat.

"Nice touch." Phoebe grinned. "Mum loves chocolate."

"Since she's your mother, I assumed she would." He laughed lightly.

They walked to the front door, and pausing, shared a nervous smile before Phoebe knocked.

The door opened within seconds. Mrs. Halliday was a diminutive woman with a kind, but slightly anxious smile. "Come in, come in!" she urged, hugging Phoebe and then turning to him. "It's so nice to meet you," she said, standing awkwardly for a moment before finally stretching up to give him a hug as well.

"It's my pleasure to meet you, Mrs. Halliday."

"Oh, please call me Susan."

He smiled. "Thank you. I brought these for you." He held out the box.

Susan grinned brightly. "You're quite the smart man, aren't you?" She chuckled before motioning for them to go inside.

Nicholas followed her and Phoebe into a cosy living room. He sat on an old dark green settee beside Phoebe, while Susan sat in a matching recliner. All the little knickknacks around the room fascinated him, and he studied them while Phoebe led the conversation, while ensuring he interacted enough not to appear rude. There were tea cups with matching saucers, ornaments and all sorts of vases. He'd never seen anything so quaint yet homey. His family home would have been considered a mansion compared to Susan's home, but he felt far more relaxed here already.

Before long, Susan invited them to sit at the table set for three. The room had yellow walls and white countertops, and the small, square table in the middle of the room was covered with a cheerful blue gingham cloth. She fussed over them, and Phoebe offered to help.

"Thank you, dear, but it's all in hand. Take a seat." She placed a dish of homemade lasagna that smelled divine in the middle of the table, along with a salad and baby potatoes. Light lace curtains floated in the breeze at the open window. It was so unpretentious, Nicholas began to relax.

"Would you mind giving thanks, Nicholas?" Susan asked after removing her apron and joining them at the table.

His mouth went dry and he swallowed hard. Although praying had become a regular part of his life, he'd never given thanks in front of anyone other than Phoebe. What if he made a mess of it in front of her mother? He was trying so hard to impress her. But he couldn't refuse—that would be worse. "Of course," he replied, sounding more confident than he felt.

Phoebe and Susan extended their hands. He took Phoebe's in his left hand and Susan's in his right. If only Alden and Charity could see him now.

He gave a nervous smile. "Let's pray." Bowing his head, he paused. He needed to get this right. *Pray from your heart...* The words were loud and clear. Yes, that's all he had to do. He didn't need to impress anyone. He drew a slow breath and began. "Lord God, thank You for Your goodness and grace.

We're truly grateful to be sharing this meal together and we ask that You bless our time around this table. In Jesus' name. Amen." Grabbing Phoebe's hand quickly again after she let go, he continued. "Oh, and please bless this food and the hands that prepared it. Amen."

His quick cover elicited small chuckles from both Phoebe and her mum, but he wasn't embarrassed. Instead, he felt strengthened for having been able to pray in front of these two special women.

Throughout the dinner, Susan continued to make small, complimentary remarks. She noted how caring he was towards Phoebe and the genuine concern he showed for her. "Phoebe told me that one of the first things she noticed about you in Thailand was your humility. To think at that point she didn't even know who you were! I can see she was right. You really are a humble young man."

His heart, along with his face, warmed. He'd never been complimented for being humble before. "Thank you. I haven't always been like that, but I certainly hope that I'm growing to be more Christ-like." He'd learned a lot of the language used in Christian circles. Sometimes he still felt he was faking it and the words were uncomfortable on his tongue, but he wanted to continue to grow, and people had been gracious to him during this time of exploration and learning.

Once the main course was finished, Susan brought out a delicious home-baked apple pie with ice cream, and then they adjourned to the living room for coffee.

Later, when they were leaving, Susan took his hand and gazed deep into his eyes. "Well, Nicholas, I'm thrilled to have finally met you. I do hope you'll visit again. You'd be welcome at any time."

"Thank you. I'd like that very much." Smiling at Phoebe's mum, he wondered what he'd been so anxious about.

Phoebe grinned at both of them, and then, after hugging her mother, slipped her hand into his as they walked to his car. "So how was it?" she asked after settling onto the seat.

"Not half as frightening as I thought it would be." He chuckled.

"I'm glad to hear that." Her smile lit up her face.

"Your mother is lovely. Just like you."

"And she thought you weren't half bad! You really impressed her, Nick."

He was so relieved. Desperately wanting her mum to like him, hearing that she did made all the difference in the world. "I'm so glad, Phoebe."

As their gazes met and held, his heart thudded. Leaning towards her, he lifted his hand and cupped her cheek before brushing his lips against hers. Unable to stop himself, he pressed harder. Her eager response surprised him, and he could have stayed there forever, kissing her, but her mum was standing on the verandah, waiting to wave them off. He pulled away, although he had a burning desire, an aching need, to never let her go.

"I hope your mum didn't see that." They glanced over at the house. Susan was indeed on the verandah, an impish grin on her face.

"I'm sure she's happy about it." Phoebe laughed as she lowered the window and waved to her mum while Nick reversed the car down the driveway.

What an incredible night! Nicholas drove Phoebe home in a haze of joy, hardly believing what had happened. Reaching her apartment, he pulled up and parked, and before he climbed out to walk her to her door, he pulled her close and kissed her again, savouring every moment. Aware of the need to exercise restraint, he pulled away but feather-touched her lips with his, not wanting the moment to end. Finally, he straightened. "Come on, I'll walk you to your door."

She leaned into him as they strolled across the moonlit grass.

"It was a wonderful evening, Phoebe. Thank you."

"It was amazing," she said, dreamily.

Reaching the entry, he turned her towards him. As she gazed up at him, he was tempted to kiss her long and hard, but instead, he cupped her cheeks in his hands and kissed her softly. "Good night, Phoebe."

"Good night, Nick."

She went inside and Nicholas returned to his car, thanking God for everything that had occurred that night.

CHAPTER 19

A week had passed since Phoebe took Nick to meet her mother. She was still riding on the excitement of that evening and couldn't believe that she and Nick had finally kissed. And since then, they'd kissed again, several times, but he'd remained a perfect gentleman and hadn't expected more from her, despite her being aware of his growing desire.

She put her hair up and added a touch of lip gloss to her makeup in anticipation of his arrival. When the doorbell rang, Phoebe buzzed him up.

"Hey." Smiling, he pulled her close and kissed her tenderly.

As much as she would have liked to stand there kissing him all night, she pulled away and invited him in.

"How was your day?" he asked casually.

"It was great. Michael's finally getting most three-letter words. I'm so proud of him." Michael was a little boy in her class who'd been struggling with his reading.

"That's awesome. I knew you'd be able to help him."

Phoebe loved the way Nick was always so positive with her, but she often wondered what *his* days at work were like. Since he always remained vague when she asked, she sensed that he preferred to leave that stuff at the office rather than discuss it after hours.

"So, what's the plan for tonight?" she asked as she returned to her desk and closed down her computer.

"A surprise." He grinned impishly.

Phoebe laughed. She'd come to love Nick's surprises, but tonight, something made her wonder if he was planning to propose. Her stomach fluttered. Lately, she'd been thinking so much about her future with him, but they'd only been together four months, so she couldn't imagine he was ready to jump at marriage so soon. She put the thought away. "Okay, I'm ready for whatever!"

He grabbed her hand and led her out the door. They strolled to the car, and once seated, he headed out of the city.

"Okay, now I'm really curious. Where are we going?" All she could see was sand, and no lights, other than moonlight, reflecting on the glistening Pacific Ocean.

"Just wait," he told her, winking.

Before long, lights twinkled in the distance. As the car slowed, a white gazebo came into view. It was decorated with fairy lights, like on a Christmas tree. Her heart fluttered; she was speechless. A small table with a candle flickering in the middle drew her attention. The whole thing was set up for just the two of them.

"Nick, this is so beautiful," she said breathlessly, kicking off her shoes.

He grinned as he grabbed her hand and led her across the

sand to the table. The salty sea air filled her nostrils and played softly through her hair. The scene was magical, and exactly how any woman would wish to be proposed to. And yet, they hadn't spoken of marriage.

Reaching the table, he pulled a chair out for her, and then sat opposite. A waiter, dressed in a suit and bow tie, approached and welcomed them.

"Good evening, Mr. Barrington and Miss Halliday. I am your waiter for this evening, and I am at your beck and call. Whatever you wish, please let me know." He turned and addressed Phoebe. "However, Mr. Barrington has instructed the chef to prepare your favourite dishes, which will be served in small courses. To start with, may I pour you a glass of wine?"

Phoebe hesitated. She didn't normally drink alcohol, but maybe one glass wouldn't hurt. But could she trust herself? No, it was safer to stick with a non-alcoholic beverage. She smiled at the waiter. "May I please have a non-alcoholic apple cider?"

"Of course. I'll be right back. And you, sir? What can I get for you?"

"I'll have the same, thanks."

"You're more than welcome."

After he stepped away, Phoebe leaned in closer and gazed into Nick's eyes. "This is magnificent, Nick. Thank you."

He reached out and stroked her hand. "It's a special night, Phoebe."

Her stomach turned in anticipation. "Really?"

"You don't know what today is?"

She frowned, but nothing came to mind. Had she gotten it wrong and this was for some other occasion entirely?

"It's been exactly four months since our first date," he said softly.

All the air rushed from her lungs. Of course! It was their four-month anniversary! How could she have forgotten?

"And exactly seven months since the day we met."

"You remember all of that?"

"Of course I do. Should I be embarrassed?"

"Not at all. I'm impressed. I didn't realise what the day was," she confessed, feeling bad. "But I'm so glad you remembered."

"You've made such a lasting impact on me, Phoebe. I'll never forget any of our days together."

She exhaled a long sigh of contentment. Although Nick's words were smooth, she knew he was genuine. His honesty was even more integral than his charm. He wasn't about to propose, and no matter how much she would have liked it, she didn't mind. Their time would come. And Nick would certainly do it in a way that was special, of that she was sure.

The waiter returned with their drinks and the first course of their Thai banquet.

Nick took her hand and gave thanks. Hearing him pray with such sincerity warmed her heart so.

As they ate, soft music played in the background, and they chatted easily about many things, but most of all, their time in Thailand. After they finished eating, Nick took her hand and led her to the side of the gazebo where two recliners, complete with cushions and rugs, had been positioned perfectly to gaze at the water and the sky. Seated on the recliners, they leaned back and gazed at the stars together. Holding Nick's hand, Phoebe felt entirely at peace.

"The stars are amazing, aren't they?" Nick's gentle voice floated on the air.

"Yes, they are."

Still staring at the sky, he asked, "Where in the world would you go if there were no limits and you could go anywhere?"

She pondered for a moment. She'd dreamed of travelling the world. Ireland was on top of her list, as were the heather-filled highlands of Scotland, the monasteries of Ethiopia, and the jungles of Ecuador. But where did she want to go more than anywhere else? She finally replied, "I think I'd want to go back to Thailand. I can't get all those children out of my mind. Of all the places I'd love to see, nothing would please me more than to return there and spend time with the children at the mission."

"I can't blame you. I've been to a lot of places and had many opportunities to travel, but that's where I'd want to go, too."

"I wish I could do more work there. When I think back to my time at the mission, I realise now how much more I could have done," Phoebe admitted.

Nick shifted in his seat and turned to her. "Well, I have a surprise for you."

Phoebe met his gaze and waited. His eyes twinkled, and she grew curious.

"Your school year is almost over, right?" he asked.

"Yes," she replied cautiously.

"Good. Because I think we should go back, but not on our own." His face grew animated. "Let's take a team from church. Fully funded, of course. I'm sure they'll love it."

"A team from church? Fully funded?" Phoebe repeated.

"Yes. It would be my pleasure."

"Nick, that's amazing!" She threw her arms around him, almost causing the recliners to fall over.

He laughed. "It's my honour, Phoebe. I'm glad to do it."

"I'm speechless, Nick. I can hardly believe it! You'd really pay for a team from church to go to Bangkok?"

"Yes. And invite your mum to come as well."

"Really?"

Nodding, he raised his hand to her cheek and gently pulled her face towards his. With his lips lightly brushing hers, and the sound of waves lapping the shore, Phoebe thought she was in heaven.

Later, they strolled along the shoreline arm in arm, and then, when the time came to leave, he drove her home, and although he hadn't proposed, she felt entirely satisfied with the evening.

CHAPTER 20

*I*t took two months to prepare for the trip to Thailand, but Nick was beyond excited when the team of thirteen boarded the plane for Bangkok. Susan, Phoebe's mum, was among the group, and he knew she'd love the country as much as her daughter did. It would be exciting for them to be on this journey together.

Ten hours later, Thomas and Judy met the group at the airport. Nick was overjoyed to see them again.

"Great to see you, Nick! Hopefully this time we can meet the real you!" Thomas winked as he clapped Nick on the back. "I hope it wasn't too hard to take time off?"

Nick let out a small chuckle. "Thankfully, everything is finally sorted." He was actually very relieved that they'd been able to rectify the situation and the client was happy. The business had made itself a media target, but by bringing the issue into the open and dealing with it promptly, they'd avoided the worst, and they'd even been praised for their ethical approach.

"I'm glad to hear it. I wish I could say we have plenty for you to do, but it's the strangest thing. After your visit, we suddenly had a major spike in donor activity and now we have a full-time handy-man," Thomas said, winking again. When Nick had contacted Thomas about this trip, Thomas had confessed that he'd known from the beginning who he was but had decided to honour Nick's desire for anonymity.

"Well, I'm still Nick. Same man, just a few details are different. I hope no one treats me any differently than they did before."

"They won't. Everyone's excited to see you again, and aside from Judy and myself, no one will have any clue about the difference between the bearded Nick and the billionaire Nicholas. They're just excited to see you."

Nick smiled. "And I'll be glad to see them."

"Now, are you going to introduce us to everyone?" Thomas asked.

"Sure. You obviously remember Phoebe." Nick placed his hand on the small of her back, his heart warming as she smiled at him.

"How could we forget?" Thomas leaned in and gave her a hug. Judy followed suit.

"And this is Susan, her mum."

They both smiled and shook hands with her. Nick then introduced the rest of the team before they boarded the mini bus and were driven to the hostel Nick had booked for them. He'd been tempted to book a five-star hotel, but finally decided on a hostel near the mission. It was still comfortable and better suited the purpose of the trip than a fancy hotel that would be considered extravagant under the circumstances.

That night, the team, along with Thomas and Judy, enjoyed a meal at a nearby Thai restaurant. Being back in this vibrant city was beyond wonderful, and being there with Phoebe made it even more special. Nick was so pleased that this trip had come to fruition, not just to work at the mission, but to share the experience with Phoebe. He thanked God every day for bringing her into his life; he couldn't deny the fact that he was falling head over in heels in love with her. She was everything he'd ever wanted in a woman—bright, bubbly and humble, and she didn't care one iota about his money. But more than that, she lived her faith, and that fact alone made her the beautiful person she was.

The next day, after an early breakfast at the hostel, the team arrived at the mission ready for work. Following an introductory meeting presented by Thomas, they were allocated various duties. Some of the men were sent to the centre where 'Regenerate the Nations' worked to build relationships with the pimps, while most of the women went to different classrooms and spent time with the children.

Phoebe was excited to be assigned her old classroom with the younger children she'd worked with on her previous trip, and Susan was assigned to work with her. Nick accompanied Thomas to the boys' centre. During his previous trip to Thailand, he'd only visited a few times, and then it had been mainly to do odd jobs. Today he'd have the opportunity to help in the classroom.

He was directed to a class of ten to twelve-year-olds. There were only six boys, but they each welcomed him with wide smiles. He helped them with their English, and then, when they moved to the computer lab, he helped them to create and work with spreadsheets, skills that would be invaluable in the future as they sought employment, ensuring they would never be vulnerable again.

It was exciting to see the boys so enthusiastic about learning, but he'd only scratched the surface. He determined there and then to return at least once a year to help out, but that wasn't enough. They needed full-time, skilled teachers, and that would take money. Just as well he had some.

Walking back to the main centre later that day, Thomas chatted easily with Nick. "Judy and I were so pleased to hear that you gave your life to Jesus after you left here."

Nick smiled. "Yes, it all started here at the mission. I wasn't ready then, but God didn't give up on me. He kept prodding me, and one day at church with Phoebe, my eyes were finally opened and I understood that not only is Jesus God's solution for mankind's brokenness, He's the only way to find true peace and meaning in life, and I gave my heart to Him."

"That's wonderful, Nick. I can see a change in you already, and I think He has good things planned for you." Thomas clapped him on the back, and this time, Nick didn't mind. Thomas was not only a good friend, but a mentor, and he didn't seem phased at all that Nick was a billionaire. He was just an ordinary man in need of a Saviour.

Arriving at the main centre, most of the children had already left and what few remained were with the classroom helpers. When the team met together in the cafeteria for a debriefing session, everyone had amazing stories to tell, and it was only day one. They couldn't wait for day two.

Afterwards, as they made their way to dinner, Nick walked

beside Susan and asked how she was enjoying the experience so far.

She smiled. "It's been wonderful, Nick. Thanks for allowing me to come on this journey and to experience this amazing place."

He returned her smile. "It's been my pleasure, Susan. I'm so glad you're enjoying it." He cleared his throat and glanced down before lifting his gaze again. "You know, there's something else I wanted to talk to you about…"

Chuckling, she moved closer.

AFTER DINNER, the team returned to the hostel, exhausted but happy. Nick reluctantly left Phoebe to go to the room she was sharing with her mum and a few other women, while he went to the room he was sharing with three of the men. By the time he'd prepared for bed, they were snoring.

Despite the busy day, he wasn't tired and knew he wouldn't sleep, so he grabbed the small box he'd brought with him and walked outside onto the balcony. The air was balmy and humid after the air-conditioning inside, but it was more real. Just like the city itself.

Bangkok, a visual feast by day, was a hive of activity at night, but its vibrancy after dark signalled both thrill and tragedy. Under the cover of entertainment, human trafficking was carried on and was very real. Not just in Thailand, but in Guatemala, the United States, Spain, and even Sydney. It was all over the world, and it was heartbreaking.

But right now, Nick's mind was on Phoebe. Opening the box, he asked God for clarity. He wanted to be certain it was right. The right time. The right way. All of it. He needed peace about this decision. A decision that would change his life forever.

Hearing footsteps, he looked up and smiled. Phoebe had walked around the corner but hadn't seen him. The moment she did, she jumped and let out a small squeak, while lifting a hand to her chest. "Nick! What are you doing out here?"

He chuckled. "I could ask you the same question. I couldn't sleep."

"Me either," she said, sidling beside him.

He subtly tucked the box back into his pocket and slipped an arm around her shoulders. As she nestled against him, he pulled her close and kissed the top of her head.

"It's amazing having my mum here. Thank you for inviting her." Her voice was soft and sincere.

"It was my pleasure. She seems to be enjoying it so far."

Gazing out at the city lights, Nick realised his prayer was being answered. This was the time. This was the place. He took a deep breath and turned to face her. With her eyes shining and wisps of hair framing her face, she looked ethereal in the half-light. His heart pounded. "Phoebe…"

She gazed at him, her expression puzzled.

Gazing into her eyes, he was entranced by her. He lifted his hand and cupped her cheek. "I've never truly loved a woman before. But Phoebe, I've come to love you like I never imagined was possible." His chest rose and fell as the emotion of the moment swept through him.

Her eyes glistened, her gaze remained steady. "And I love you, Nick." Her voice was soft, quiet, sincere.

He lifted her hand and kissed her palm gently before

moving deftly onto one knee and retrieving the small box from his pocket. Opening it, he held it out. "Phoebe, I love you with all my heart and I want to share the rest of my life with you." He swallowed hard as he peered into her eyes. "Will you marry me?" Holding his breath, he removed the ring and held it out.

Her eyes widened, but she didn't look at the ring. Her gaze was fixed on him. She nodded as tears pooled in her eyes. "Yes, of course I'll marry you!"

He slowly slipped the ring onto her finger and then wrapped his arms around her, holding her tight while he let her response sink in. She'd said yes! She wanted to marry him! He was the happiest man alive! He pulled back and palmed her cheek before lowering his face and showering kisses around her lips. Then, his mouth found hers, and pressing hard, he kissed her passionately, her eager response surprising but pleasing him. When they finally parted, they were both breathless.

She gazed lovingly into his eyes. "I love you, Nick, and I can't wait to be your wife, but what will your family say?"

He brushed her cheek softly with his hand. "I don't care what they say, Phoebe. My siblings and I are different people with different priorities. My priorities are serving God and loving you. They wouldn't understand that."

"But I'd still like to meet them."

"I have no problem with that. But I'm warning you again… you might not like them."

"I won't know until I meet them. And everybody deserves a chance."

He chuckled. "And that's what I love about you."

They remained outside and chatted about their future

together until the night sky began to lighten, heralding a new day. "We should try to get at least an hour of sleep," he said.

"You're probably right, or else I'll be falling asleep in the classroom."

"Come on then, let's head inside, but first, let's commit our future to God."

She smiled. "Good idea."

They bowed their heads and Nick prayed, asking God's blessing over their future life together.

Later that morning, they announced their news to the team, who were all overjoyed but not surprised in the slightest.

The remaining time at the mission passed quickly, and before long, they were heading back to Australia. Thomas and Judy hugged everyone, thanking them for their help and inviting them back at any time.

"It's been our pleasure, Thomas," Nick said, shaking his friend's hand. "Coming here has changed my life, and I'll never forget it."

He smiled at both Nick and Phoebe. "God bless you both. Take care."

Nick stepped away and placed his hand on the small of Phoebe's back as they walked to the plane. Glancing at her, his heart warmed afresh. He was going to marry the girl of his dreams.

TWO DAYS LATER, Nicholas called his brother and sister into his office and told them about all the changes in his life. About how God had been working in him and that his original trip to Thailand had been a service project, not a vacation as they'd thought. He went on to explain everything that had happened since then, including his engagement to Phoebe.

Alden wore a look of disgust and disappointment. "You've gone crazy, big brother."

Charity was a little more understanding. "I've found religion, too. But I don't believe in one God. God is everything and everything is God. It's so freeing. No rules. Just love." She fanned her face with her hand and let out a small chuckle. "I hope you got some of that in Thailand, big brother. I've heard the Thai girls are very good in that department."

Anger seethed inside him. "You have no idea of what goes on over there, Charity." He could have said a lot more, but he would have been wasting his time. "I truly don't care what you both think. This is my life and I'm going to live it the way I feel is right. Phoebe and I are planning a small church wedding. You're both welcome to attend, but I'll understand if you don't."

"Everyone will think you've been swept up into a cult," Alden said with a sneer.

"They can think what they like. I know my mind, and I know what's right and good for me. And I somehow think our grandfather would approve, even if you don't."

"I wouldn't be too sure of that. I think he'd disinherit you." Alden lifted his brows. "Are you really sure about this? She's just a school teacher. She won't fit."

"Fit what?" As Nicholas stared at Alden, pity for his brother's shallowness flowed through him. It saddened him so much that he was at odds with his only family, but he'd made a choice, and that choice was to live his life for God and to marry Phoebe.

Alden shrugged. "Everything."

"Whatever." Nicholas dismissed them with a wave of the hand. He couldn't listen to them anymore. Although it was disheartening that his new relationships with God and Phoebe didn't meet with the approval of his siblings, he felt at peace. And he had work to do.

CHAPTER 21

*P*hoebe's wedding day couldn't come soon enough. Although she and Nick had planned a simple wedding, and she tried not to fuss about her gown, the flowers and the cake, she couldn't help wanting everything to be perfect. Occasionally, twinges of anxiety assailed her as the planning and preparation revived memories of another wedding that didn't happen. Holly was wonderful and encouraged her to focus not on the past, because she couldn't change that, but on the here and now. Nick loved her, it was obvious, and he would make a wonderful husband. And just because Reed had died three weeks before their wedding, it didn't mean that the same fate would repeat itself. Phoebe knew that, but she couldn't help but think about Reed on the day that fell exactly three weeks before her wedding.

Nick understood and went out of his way to make that day extra special for her. They both took the day off work and spent it on the harbour in the company's luxury yacht. He told her he didn't normally indulge in such extravagances, but just this once, he felt it was justified.

The day was amazing, just what she needed, and made her long even more to be his wife. She'd come to love and respect Nick so much. He'd taken her to meet his siblings one day not long after returning from Thailand, and she quickly saw why he'd been reluctant for her to meet them. She'd always tried to see the good in people, because after all, they were made in God's image, but Alden and Charity were so stuck-up and obnoxious that she found herself asking for forgiveness from the moment she met them. How Nick had come to be so different, she wasn't sure, but she was certainly glad he was.

At last, the day of the wedding came. From the moment she woke, Phoebe felt a deep peace about everything that was to take place, and once again, she committed her and Nick's marriage into the Lord's hands.

Holly arrived as Phoebe stepped out of the shower and greeted her with a beaming smile. "I can't believe you're going to marry a billionaire today, Phoebe. It's so exciting!"

Slipping a light dressing gown on, Phoebe laughed. "I'm finding it hard to believe, too. But it's not going to change me."

"I know it's not. You'll still be eating leftovers and vegemite sandwiches for lunch!"

Phoebe chuckled again as she towel-dried her hair.

"Come on. Sit down and let me do that for you."

Phoebe shifted to a chair and sat quietly while Holly dried her hair and then brushed it. Her thoughts drifted back to the moment she first laid eyes on Nick, and how she'd been so reluctant to even talk to him. "Thanks for being my friend, Holl. If you hadn't invited me to go on the trip, I might still be struggling to get over losing Reed."

"I never thought it would end with you marrying a billionaire, but hey! I'll take some of the credit!"

Phoebe caught Holly's gaze in the mirror and smiled at her friend. The guy she'd pinned her hopes on had moved on and now Holly was single and wondering what, or who, God had in store for her. "God is good, Holl. He's got something wonderful planned for you, I'm sure."

Holly laughed. "Probably not a billionaire, but I don't mind, as long as he loves the Lord."

"That's the most important thing. It really is. I don't care if Nick has money or not."

Holly grinned. "But you have to admit, it's an added bonus…"

Phoebe spun around in the chair and laughed. "I guess it is."

The buzzer sounded, indicating that someone was at the door. Phoebe glanced at the intercom panel. "It's the hairdresser. Come on, let's get this show on the road!"

Two hours later, after Phoebe's hair had been styled and her makeup done, her mother and Holly helped her into her softly flowing, white organza, A-line sweetheart gown. As she slipped it on, she felt like a princess. It was gorgeous.

"You look beautiful." Her mother brushed tears from her eyes. "Your father would have been so proud."

Despite the mention of her father, who'd died in a work accident when she was very young, Phoebe couldn't help but smile. She was so excited she was about to marry Nick.

Although she hardly remembered her father, she wished he could have been there, but she sensed he was looking down on her and laughing about how his little girl had snagged such a wonderful husband.

She stood and faced the mirror while Holly and her mum adjusted the dress. It fit perfectly, her hair was exactly how she wanted it, mainly up but with soft tendrils framing her face, and her makeup was flawless. She was ready, and she couldn't have loved her groom any more than she did right then.

Entering the church on her mother's arm, Phoebe caught sight of Nick standing at the end of the aisle, and the joy she felt was beyond measure. He looked so incredibly handsome in his light grey tuxedo. When their gazes met, the cheeky grin on his face put her completely at ease. Life would never be boring with Nick.

It was hard to tear her gaze from him as she walked slowly down the aisle, but she managed to turn her head and smile at her friends from school and church, and also at Judy, who'd flown over from Thailand for the wedding. Thomas stood proudly beside Nick as his best man.

When she reached Nick, her mother stepped away, and he took her hand and squeezed it. It was the most wonderful moment. The beginning of her new life. She smiled at him and once again was wrapped in the love flowing from his gorgeous eyes.

The ceremony began with a prayer and a short message about marriage, love, and respect. Phoebe tried her best to listen attentively. She knew it was important, but it was all so surreal. Finally, their pastor invited them to make their vows.

Taking her hand, Nick looked deep into her eyes. Her whole being seemed to be filled with waiting; the prolonged anticipation was almost unbearable, but this was the most important part of the ceremony, the part where they committed to love each other for the rest of their lives.

He took a slow breath and began. "Phoebe, I promise to love you always. I promise to do my very best to love you as Christ loves the church, to make self-sacrificing decisions for your benefit and for the good of our future family. For all our days, I'll be your beloved, and you will be mine."

Phoebe was struck not only by the sincerity in his voice, but the adoration in his eyes. He truly loved her, and she knew beyond doubt that this was the man she was to spend her life with.

Then it was her turn. After swallowing hard and taking a moment to compose herself, she looked into his eyes and began. "Nicholas, I promise to respect you always. I'll do everything in my power to meet your needs, physical, emotional and spiritual. I promise to honour you as the church honours Christ, and to trust that you have my best interests at heart at all times. I promise to love and cherish you, for richer and poorer, in sickness and in health, until death do us part, and to raise our family in the midst of that, to the glory of God alone."

She took a slow breath and held Nick's gaze before they exchanged rings and the pastor declared them husband and wife. Her heart danced with excitement as Nick kissed her with so much passion she felt heady.

The cheering and clapping from the congregation grew louder, and finally he released her. They shared a smile before facing their friends and being introduced as Mr. and Mrs. Nicholas and Phoebe Barrington. She liked the sound of that.

A small wedding breakfast followed in the fellowship hall. They'd discussed having a more lavish affair, but they both agreed that this was what they wanted.

Later, as he led her around the floor in their first dance together as a married couple, he whispered in her ear, "You look scrumptious, Mrs. Barrington."

"And so do you. I love that tux." She winked.

She could see desire in his eyes and knew he was looking forward to being alone with her that evening. She was so glad she'd made the decision to wait her whole life for this moment. To be one with her husband and honour God at the same time was worth waiting for.

At the end of the dance, the cake was brought out and after cutting it, they fed one another a piece, a sweet reminder of their commitment to provide for one another and a symbol of their love and adoration. Not that it was needed. Phoebe was already more than convinced of Nick's devotion and love.

Although eager to be by themselves, they spent a little more time at the reception with their friends before leaving. There was something truly wonderful about being surrounded by those who loved them and wanted to celebrate their union. Phoebe gave thanks to God time and time again throughout the day for all the blessings He was pouring over them.

But soon, they both knew it was time. They bid goodbye to their guests and made their way outside. Following behind, everyone cheered and clapped.

Nick opened the door of the limousine for her and then climbed in beside her, pulling her close and kissing her again to the amusement of those watching. As the limousine slowly pulled away, they paused long enough to wave to everyone before returning to where they left off.

Brushing some loose hair off her cheek, Nick gazed into her eyes and smiled. "Alone, at last."

CHAPTER 22

They spent their first night in the penthouse of the Viridian Hotel at Darling Harbour. Nick was pleased that Phoebe had allowed him to spoil her. He loved that she didn't care about 'things', that she would have been happy to spend their first night in a caravan or a tent, but he wanted to spoil her on their special day.

The penthouse had everything they could possibly need, and after arriving, they enjoyed all that the first night of a marriage should entail.

The following morning, Nick woke early and gazed at his beautiful wife. The thought of waking up beside Phoebe every morning was a dream come true. He was so blessed.

She stirred, and opening her eyes, smiled up at him. "Good morning."

He returned her smile, and so overwhelmed with love, lowered his mouth and kissed her slowly.

Later, he told her they needed to get ready to leave.

She looked at him with a pleading expression. "You're not going to tell me where we're going?"

"Nope. You just have to trust me." He grinned.

"Do we have time for breakfast?"

"Sure. I'll have it brought up while we get ready."

It didn't take long for the gourmet breakfast to be delivered, and as they enjoyed it on the balcony overlooking the glistening harbour, they talked about the future, all of the dreams they had, the fact that they wanted to spend at least one month out of every year in Thailand, and how they might manage that when they had a family.

Nick was so excited to see how Phoebe responded to everything. She seemed overjoyed and thrilled at the prospects ahead of them. He couldn't wait to give her everything that he'd always dreamed of giving a wife.

With breakfast finished, they left the hotel and Nick drove them to the airfield where his family's private jet was kept. Given all that he'd gone through with his siblings, he'd struggled with the decision to use the jet, but finally had felt at peace about it. He was only getting married once, after all. Alden and Charity had given him a hard time over the decision, but he'd expected that. They didn't support his marriage, but Nick prayed that in time they would come around, and that like him, they too would discover the love of Jesus and realise their priorities had been wrong.

Reaching the airfield, Nick spoke with the pilot who told him he still had a few things to prep before they left. "I won't be long, but you might want to grab a coffee," Roger said.

Nick led Phoebe into the waiting area and poured freshly brewed coffee into two mugs.

Grabbing the morning paper, his eyes shot open as he scanned the front-page headline.

Billionaire Marries Teacher. Barrington Family Absent.

He groaned. How had their wedding made the front page? There was even a photo of him and Phoebe leaving the church. Someone must have been across the street taking photos.

He blew out an annoyed breath but tried to brush the intrusion off. He didn't want this ruining their honeymoon. More than anything, he wanted to get to their honeymoon destination so they could enjoy their time together and indulge in all the relaxation and sun they could ever want before returning to real life.

He guessed that Phoebe had seen the headline as well, but she wasn't upset. He appreciated the way she always tried to keep an even temper, and he knew that she'd cope with whatever challenges came her way by being married to him. It made him admire and love her even more.

Before long, Roger stepped into the waiting area and told them everything was ready and it was time to go.

Nick held Phoebe's hand as they walked across the tarmac and boarded the jet.

As the plane ascended, she asked if he was finally going to tell her where they were going.

He grinned. "Not yet."

"Why not? We're already on our way!" she urged, excitedly.

He gave in. After all, it wouldn't be too long before they arrived, so she might as well know. "Alright then." He gazed into her eyes, waiting for her reaction. "For the next three weeks, we'll be on our very own, private, secluded island in the South Pacific."

The announcement had the effect he'd hoped for. Phoebe's delight was evident from the way her eyes sparkled and her mouth dropped open. "Our own private island?"

"Totally private. A chef will come each day and prepare our meals, but other than him, we don't need to see anyone unless we want to. We can take a boat to another island about twenty minutes away, but if we don't want to leave, everything we need will be on our island."

"For three whole weeks?"

"Yes. Three weeks in paradise. Alone. You packed your swimsuit, right?"

"Of course! You told me we were going to a beach, but I thought it might be somewhere in the Whitsundays. I never imagined this!"

Nick took her hand, and bringing it to his lips, kissed it softly. "I'm so glad you're excited. It's going to be wonderful."

THE ISLAND WAS AMAZING. A small dot in the middle of an azure sea, covered with palm trees and white sand. Despite the tropical heat, a gentle sea breeze greeted them as they disembarked the jet. Roger drove them to their bungalow in a four-wheeled ATV, and then, after carrying their bags inside, promised to return in three weeks' time.

"Thanks, Roger. You're the best." Nick clapped the pilot on the back in a friendly manner. Not how Phoebe would have expected a billionaire to treat a member of staff, but then, Nick was different.

After Roger left, Nick pulled her into his arms and kissed

her passionately. "Well, Mrs. Barrington. What are we going to do?"

She laughed at the grin that spread across his face. She knew exactly what he wanted to do, but she ducked under his arm and sprinted for the beach. She laughed as he chased after her. Just as she reached the water, he caught up and grabbed hold of her. They landed, arms around each other, in the clear, warm water. Lowering his mouth, he brushed his lips over hers and grinned. "There's nowhere to run to, my love."

The next three weeks were bliss. Phoebe couldn't have asked for a more romantic honeymoon, and by the time they returned to Sydney, she knew beyond doubt that hers and Nick's futures were safe in God's hands.

EPILOGUE

*E*ight months later

     "I don't understand how you can give all of this up, Nicholas." Although Charity spoke in a clipped tone, Phoebe sensed she'd be saying a whole lot more to her brother if she wasn't there.

It was Nick's last day of work, and Phoebe had come into the office to help him finish packing his things.

"I've never felt fulfilled doing this. You know that. I like the work, but it doesn't fulfill me. Neither does the money. I've made my decision," he said firmly, his gaze steady.

"Well, I'm going to miss you," Charity muttered, absently picking at an imaginary piece of fluff on the arm of a chair.

Nick stopped what he was doing and walked slowly towards her. Slipping his arms around her, he looked into her eyes. "I'm going to miss you, too, Charity."

Phoebe struggled to contain her tears as Charity let Nick hug her. Alden had already told him that he'd have nothing to do with him, so this was an unexpected breakthrough and would give Nick hope that he wasn't about to totally lose his complete family.

"Make sure you come by occasionally."

"We will," he replied. "Take care, Charity."

Nick let her go and picked up the last box.

She nodded and watched as he and Phoebe left the office for the last time.

"Are you okay?" Phoebe asked as they waited for the elevator.

"Yes."

She smiled at him. "I'm proud of you, Nick." In their eight months of marriage, a lot had happened for them both. They'd moved to the suburbs and found a home that, although small, was large enough for not only the two of them, but also for two children. If they had more, they might have to size up, but they weren't concerned at this point in time since they weren't expecting yet.

He was giving up so much, but he kept assuring her that he was gaining so much more. Her, for a start. They were growing closer every day. And then there was their church family who'd embraced him with open arms and hearts. Phoebe loved watching him grow in his faith, and despite the pain she knew he felt by being disowned by his family, she also knew how much he was looking forward to their future. Nick still had his money in savings and stocks, securely put away, but they'd decided to live on an average income.

And now, they were starting a new venture. Nick had decided to use a large portion of his funds to start a new company. A company selling products made by former trafficking victims so that those who'd finished school and were able could be well employed, helping to prevent the cycle of trafficking with their own children.

In addition to providing jobs, they were also heavily supporting organisations like 'Regenerate the Nations' and 'Hesed', and others that their new employees had gone through.

They'd already made one visit to Thailand, Cambodia, and the Philippines to get their company started and to partner with organisations through whom they could hire their artisans. With Nick's business mindset and Phoebe's love for people, they were already making inroads.

Phoebe had decided not to return to teaching so she could devote herself full time to the business. She was sad to leave a job she loved, but was thrilled about the opportunities ahead and the difference they would be making.

The elevator arrived and they stepped inside.

"Are you sure you're okay?" she asked.

"I'm doing great."

"Even with the loss of the job and family?"

He nodded. *"For what does it profit a man to gain the whole world and forfeit his soul?"* He quoted from Mark chapter eight.

Phoebe stretched to her tippy toes and kissed him on the lips. He was right. He was losing a lot, but the call of Christ was to die to self. And by dying to self, he had gained eternal life. Nothing on earth could top that.

A NOTE FROM THE AUTHOR

I hope you enjoyed "Her Kind-Hearted Billionaire" as much as I enjoyed writing it. There are/will be at least three more books in the "Billionaires with Heart Christian Romance Series", so don't miss them!

"Her Generous Billionaire" is the story of Marcus, a self-made billionaire widower, and Tiffany, a divorced solo mum, and you can grab it here.

To make sure you don't miss it, and to be notified of all my new releases, why not join my Readers' list by going to http://www.julietteduncan.com/subscribe to subscribe? You'll also receive a free thank-you copy of "Hank and Sarah - A Love Story", a clean love story with God at the center.

Enjoyed "Her Kind-Hearted Billionaire"? You can make a big difference. Help other people find this book by writing a review and telling them why you liked it. Honest reviews of my books help bring them to the attention of other readers just like yourself, and I'd be very grateful if you could spare just five minutes to leave a review (it can be as short as you like) on the book's Amazon page.

Oh, and don't forget to keep reading for a bonus chapter of "Her Generous Billionaire". I think you'll enjoy it.

Blessings,
Juliette

Her Generous Billionaire

Chapter 1

Sydney, Australia

The onions needed a little longer. Marcus Alcott placed the lid on the pot to let them simmer further before adding the chicken and other vegetables to the meal he was cooking for himself and his seventy-one-year-old mother, Ruth. The tantalising aroma of the onions made his stomach rumble, but he was a patient man, and he'd wait until they were cooked to perfection.

He turned as his mother wheeled herself into the kitchen. Bending down, Marcus kissed her soft cheek. "Hello Mum. How was your study?" Ruth suffered from severe arthritis but it didn't stop her from attending her weekly Bible Study group.

"Wonderful as always, dear," she replied in her sweet voice. "Something smells nice. What are you cooking?"

"Your favourite. Stir-fried chicken and vegetables."

"You do spoil me, Marcus." His mother's eyes twinkled as she wheeled closer. "What can I do to help?"

"It's all in hand, Mum. Just relax."

"Okay. Thank you, love." She shifted back, giving him space. A few moments later she asked, "Do you remember Stacie Templeton?"

Marcus ran a hand through his thick, brown hair. His mum knew so many people, but he thought he remembered her. "I think so."

"Well, she mentioned that her daughter's company is catering for the annual Breast Cancer Fundraising Ball this year."

Marcus stiffened as a shudder raced up his spine. He knew what was coming next.

"Have you decided who you're taking?" His mother quirked a brow.

Trying to appear distracted, he quickly turned to the pot and lifted the lid and inspected the onions again.

"Marcus?"

He blew out a breath. "No, Mum. Not yet." Tipping the diced chicken into the pan, he grabbed a spatula and combined the chicken with the browned onions. "I'm working on it."

"Good. Make sure you do. I'll set the table."

As his mother disappeared into the adjoining dining room of the harbour-side mansion they shared, a relieved sigh escaped his lips. Why would any woman want to accompany him to a ball honouring his late wife? Bree, his childhood sweetheart and the love of his life, had succumbed to the insidious disease five years earlier. He was now the main patron of the fund-raising event, an event which always revived memories of his beautiful wife who'd been taken too soon. He went through this same dilemma every year. Who would he invite?

Despite the memories it invoked, he loved the ball. The money raised funded research so other men needn't suffer the devastating loss he had. If only he could go on his own, but he was expected to take a partner—attending a ball on one's own was frowned upon in his social circle. He blew out another breath. He'd have to think who to invite soon, otherwise his mum would choose for him, and that could be disastrous.

His mother only wanted him to be happy again. He knew that. And although he didn't want to be alone for the rest of his life, he couldn't imagine marrying again, even though it was something his mother so clearly wanted. The very idea was painful and seemed unreasonable, even impossible.

They both knew what it was like to lose a spouse. Bree had succumbed to cancer, and his father had been killed by a teen drunk driver. Losing a spouse was an ache no one ever truly recovered from, but Ruth Alcott had done her best over the past ten years to live her life to the fullest, despite her loss and ailing health. She had no desire to marry again, but it didn't stop her from wishing Marcus would.

"Shall I add some peri-peri to the chicken?" he called out.

"Not tonight, dear. My stomach's a little sensitive today," his mum replied. Marcus grinned. It was the same answer she always gave. He'd add the spice separately to his own meal, like he always did.

As he continued cooking, memories of that day ten years

earlier crossed his mind. He'd been at work when the call came from the police. He rushed home to find his mum a weeping mess. The young woman, Sally Hubbard, had been arrested, but his dad was dead. He'd died instantly, and to begin with, neither Marcus nor his mum could believe it. Sally was sentenced and spent three years in jail for dangerous driving causing death. During that time, Marcus and Ruth came to forgive the young woman who displayed deep remorse over her actions.

She still came around now and then to visit his mum. It was a strange relationship, and each time they saw her, memories were revived and their forgiveness tested. But as Christians, it was what they were called to do, so despite their sadness and loss, they forgave her and were kind to her.

Marcus exhaled a deep sigh as he scooped the stir fry onto two plates and turned the gas off. This wasn't the life he'd imagined he'd be living right now. He and Bree had hoped for at least two children, but that had never eventuated. He didn't regret living with his mother—they provided companionship for each other, but sometimes he felt saddened by what might have been.

He carried the plates into the dining room, placing them onto the table before helping his mum into her ergonomic dining chair. He then filled two glasses with sparkling water and a squirt of lime juice.

"This looks lovely, dear." She smiled sweetly at him.

"Thanks, Mum." Returning her smile, Marcus took her hand and prayed over the meal, thanking God for all their blessings as well as the food before them. Despite having more money than he could ever need or use, he was very conscious that everything he had came from the Lord, and besides, after a busy day at work, it was always good to pause for a moment and settle his thoughts.

Letting go of his mother's hand, he sipped his water before adding some spiced seasoning to his meal. He'd just taken his first mouthful when she waved her fork in the air. She was mulling something over, and he knew what it was.

"I've been thinking a lot about the charity ball," she said, toying with her food.

His mother was far from manipulative, but she was an expert at getting him to listen even when he didn't want to. It had been a long day, and although his I.T. company practically ran itself, he still invested much time ensuring it continued to move forward. That involved detailed planning and long-winded meetings. Sensing his day was far from over, he took a deep breath and waited to hear what it was that she might have to say.

"What have you been thinking, Mum?"

"That you ought to invite Tiffany."

He blinked. "Tiffany?"

"Yes. She's a lovely young woman, and it would do her good to go out and enjoy herself. She's such a hard worker. And she's also quite beautiful," his mother added, her eyes twinkling.

Marcus inhaled deeply. He'd never thought of his mother's part-time caregiver as someone he might invite to an important event like the gala charity ball. Nothing against the woman; he'd just never considered her in that way. He did have to agree with his mother, though. Tiffany was attractive. But she was their employee. How could he invite her to the ball? No matter that she was an excellent caregiver to his mother, Tiffany was still…an employee. And he knew very little about her. Not that taking her would mean that it was a date. But what if she considered it was a date and it caused confusion in the future? Wasn't that why he hadn't invited any of the women from church? Because he didn't want them to get the wrong idea?

"I don't know about that, Mum. Don't you think it would be confusing? I mean, we hired her to do a job. If she's suddenly asked by her employer to be his date for the night, don't you think she might feel manipulated? Or that she'd get the wrong idea?"

"Oh, come now, Marcus. She'd understand. You can tell her she's doing you a favour, and I'm sure she'd be a wonderful companion for the evening."

He wasn't sure. Maybe he could ask her. Ensure she understood it was just for one evening. Like she was working. But still, it didn't entirely make sense that this was a good idea. It could cause problems. And even if it didn't, did he want to go to an event honouring his late wife with his mother's caregiver?

"I'll consider it," he promised. But as he ate his meal, he concluded that the idea was next to impossible. It simply wouldn't work.

Continue reading! You can order your copy now. Release date: 18 June 2019

A Time for Everything Series

A Time For Everything Series is a mature-age contemporary Christian romance series set in Sydney, Australia and Texas, USA. If you like real-life characters, faith-filled families, and friendships that become something more, then you'll love these inspirational second-chance romances.

The True Love Series

Set in Australia, what starts out as simple love story grows into a family saga, including a dad battling bouts of depression and guilt, an ex-wife with issues of her own, and a young step-mum trying to mother a teenager who's confused and hurting. Through it all, a love story is woven. A love story between a caring God and His precious children as He gently draws them to Himself and walks with them through the trials and joys of life.

"A beautiful Christian story. I enjoyed all of the books in this series. They all brought out Christian concepts of faith in action."

"Wonderful set of books. Weaving the books from story to story. Family living, God, & learning to trust Him with all their hearts."

The Precious Love Series

The Precious Love Series continues the story of Ben, Tessa and Jayden from the The True Love Series, although each book can be read on its own. All of the books in this series will warm your heart and draw you closer to the God who loves and cherishes you without condition.

"I loved all the books by Juliette, but those about Jaydon and Angie's stories are my favorites...can't wait for the next one..."

"Juliette Duncan has earned my highest respect as a Christian romance writer. She continues to write such touching stories about real life and the tragedies, turmoils, and joys that happen while we are living. The words that she uses to write about her characters relationships with God can only come from someone that has had a very close & special with her Lord and Savior herself. I have read all of her books and if you are a reader of Christian fiction books I would highly recommend her books." Vicki

The Shadows Series

An inspirational romance, a story of passion and love, and of God's inexplicable desire to free people from pasts that haunt them so they can live a life full of His peace, love and forgiveness, regardless of the circumstances. Book 1, *"Lingering Shadows"* is set in England, and follows the story of Lizzy, a headstrong, impulsive young lady from a privileged background, and Daniel, a roguish Irishman who sweeps her off her feet. But can Lizzy leave the shadows of her past behind and give Daniel the love he deserves, and will Daniel find freedom and release in God?

Hank and Sarah - A Love Story, *the Prequel to "The Madeleine Richards Series" is a FREE thank you gift for joining my mailing list. You'll also be the first to hear about my next books and get exclusive sneak previews. Get your free copy at www.julietteduncan.com/subscribe*

The Madeleine Richards Series

Although the 3 book series is intended mainly for pre-teen/ Middle Grade girls, it's been read and enjoyed by people of all ages.

"Juliette has a fabulous way of bringing her characters to life. Maddy is at typical teenager with authentic views and actions that truly make it feel like you are feeling her pain and angst. You want to enter into her situation and make everything better. Mom and soon to be dad respond to her with love and gentle persuasion while maintaining their faith and trust in Jesus, whom they know, will give them wisdom as they continue on their lives journey. Appropriate for teenage readers but any age can enjoy." Amazon Reader

The Potter's House Books...stories of hope, redemption, and second chances. Find out more here:

http://pottershousebooks.com/our-books/

The Homecoming

Kayla McCormack is a famous pop-star, but her life is a mess. Dane Carmichael has a disability, but he has a heart for God. He had a crush on her at school, but she doesn't remember him. His simple faith and life fascinate her, But can she surrender her life of fame and fortune to find true love?

Unchained

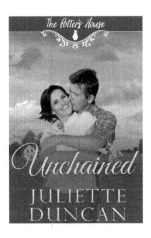

Imprisoned by greed – redeemed by love

Sally Richardson has it all. A devout, hard-working, well-respected husband, two great kids, a beautiful home, wonderful friends. Her life is perfect. Until it isn't.

When Brad Richardson, accountant, business owner, and respected church member, is sentenced to five years in jail, Sally is shell-shocked. How had she not known about her husband's fraudulent activity? And how, as an upstanding member of their tight-knit community, did he ever think he'd get away with it? He's defrauded clients, friends, and fellow church members. She doubts she can ever trust him again.

Locked up with murderers and armed robbers, Brad knows that the only way to survive his incarceration is to seek God with all his heart - something he should have done years ago. But how does he convince his family that his remorse is genuine? Will they ever forgive him?

He's failed them. But most of all, he's failed God. His poor decisions have ruined this once perfect family.

They've lost everything they once held dear. Will they lose each other as well?

Blessings of Love

She's going on mission to help others. He's going to win her heart.

Skye Matthews, bright, bubbly and a committed social work major, is the pastor's daughter. She's in love with Scott Anderson, the most eligible bachelor, not just at church, but in the entire town.

Scott lavishes her with flowers and jewellery and treats her like a lady, and Skye has no doubt that life with him would be amazing. And yet, sometimes, she can't help but feel he isn't committed enough. Not to her, but to God.

She knows how important Scott's work is to him, but she has a niggling feeling that he isn't prioritising his faith, and that concerns her. If only he'd join her on the mission trip to Burkina Faso…

Scott Anderson, a smart, handsome civil engineering graduate, has just received the promotion he's been working for for months. At age twenty-four, he's the youngest employee to ever hold a position of this calibre, and he's pumped.

Scott has been dating Skye long enough to know that she's 'the one', but just when he's about to propose, she asks him to go on mission with her. His plans of marrying her are thrown to the wind.

Can he jeopardise his career to go somewhere he's never heard of, to work amongst people he'd normally ignore?

If it's the only way to get a ring on Skye's finger, he might just risk it…

And can Skye's faith last the distance when she's confronted with a truth she never expected?

Stand Alone Christian Romantic Suspense

Leave Before He Kills You

When his face grew angry, I knew he could murder…

That face drove me and my three young daughters to flee across

Australia.

I doubted he'd ever touch the girls, but if I wanted to live and see them grow, I had to do something.

The plan my friend had proposed was daring and bold, but it also gave me hope.

My heart thumped. What if he followed?

Radical, honest and real, this Christian romantic suspense is one woman's journey to freedom you won't put down...get your copy and read it now.

ABOUT THE AUTHOR

Juliette Duncan is a Christian fiction author, passionate about writing stories that will touch her readers' hearts and make a difference in their lives. Although a trained school teacher, Juliette spent many years working alongside her husband in their own business, but is now relishing the opportunity to follow her passion for writing stories she herself would love to read. Based in Brisbane, Australia, Juliette and her husband have five adult children, eight grandchildren, and an elderly long haired dachshund. Apart from writing, Juliette loves exploring the great world we live in, and has travelled extensively, both within Australia and overseas. She also enjoys social dancing and eating out.

Connect with Juliette:

Email: juliette@julietteduncan.com

Website: www.julietteduncan.com

Facebook: www.facebook.com/JulietteDuncanAuthor

Twitter: https://twitter.com/Juliette_Duncan

Made in the USA
Lexington, KY
11 December 2019